Sons of the Sphinx

To
Jaedon-
Enjoy your visit
to Ancient Egypt!.
Cheryl

Cheryl Carpinello

Cheryl
Carpinello

Grateful acknowledgment to William Shakespeare and his creative genius for writing a story with so many memorable lines: Romeo and Juliet.

Published in Print and Ebook format by:

Cheryl Carpinello
Beyond Today Educator
http://www.beyondtodayeducator.com

First Print Edition 2014
First Ebook Edition 2014

Cover by Bernistevens Design
Edited by Nancy M. Bell
Copyedited by Louise Guillaudeu
Layout and Production by Cheryl Carpinello

Printed in the USA by Createspace
ISBN 978-1500554934

Also by Cheryl Carpinello

Sons of the Sphinx (A Quest Book)
Tutankhamen Speaks
Guinevere: On the Eve of Legend (A Quest Book)
Young Knights of the Round Table: The King's Ransom
(A Quest Book)

*Behind the Scenes of Young Knights of the Round Table:
The King's Ransom*
*King Arthur's Story from Guinevere: On the Eve of
Legend*

Picture Books:

*Grandma's Tales: What If I Came Home from the
Circus*
Wild Creatures in My Neighborhood

To Connor Joseph
Enjoy all the adventures in your life.

A special thanks to Mrs. Hegge's 2014 sixth graders for their willingness to read and comment on this story.

My gratitude to Nancy M. Bell and Louise Guillaudeu for their dedicated content and copy editing. My thanks to my online critique partners Margo Berendsen and Cecilia Ramirez. Without them, this story would not have been published.

Sons of the Sphinx

Table of Contents

Pharaohs of the Eighteenth Dynasty (1550-1295 BC)

Map of Ancient Egypt

The Prophecy

Sons of the Sphinx

Glossary of Egyptian Gods, People, Places, and Terms

To My Readers

Pharaohs of the Eighteenth Dynasty
(1550-1295 BC)

Ahmosis	1550-1525 BC
Amenhotep I	1525-1504 BC
Tuthmosis I	1504-1492 BC
Tuthmosis II	1492-1479 BC
Hatshepsut	1479-1457 BC*
Tuthmosis III	1479-1425 BC*
Amenhotep II	1427-1397 BC
Tuthmosis IV (great-grandfather of Tutankhamen)	1397-1387 BC
Amenhotep III (grandfather of Tutankhamen)	1387-1349 BC
Amenhotep IV/Akhenaten (father of Tutankhamen)	1349-1333 BC*
Smenkhkare/Neferetti (wife of Akhenaten)	1335-1333 BC*
Tutankhamen	1333-1324 BC
Ay	1324-1321 BC
Horemheb	1321-1295 BC

*denotes co-regency

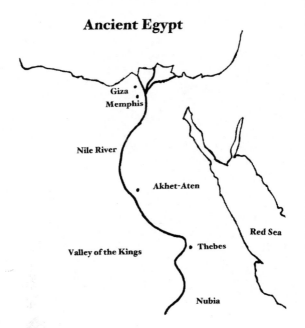

Ancient Egypt

Giza
Memphis

Nile River

Akhet-Aten

Red Sea

Valley of the Kings

Thebes

Nubia

The Prophecy

Behold, when the last boy pharaoh is awakened, he will have one chance to right the wrong. United with a spirit vessel from the future, he must seek to find the one robbed of his reign who will lead the way to the tomb of his lost queen. There must the confrontation with the usurper be held and the presentation of his confession to the old priests be given. If the usurper holds his tenth Jubilee and is allowed to acknowledge his son as his successor, the wrong will not be righted, and the queen will remain lost to her pharaoh forever.

Chapter 1

I **don't see dead people.** I hear them. I talk to them. Boy, you should try that. Talk about people looking at you like you've got two heads. That will do it. I used to look in the mirror after talking to them to see what others saw. All I saw was me, Rosa, an ordinary fifteen-year-old girl. Well, not so ordinary. I do have my father's emerald eyes, but no glowing auras, no ghosts on my shoulders, only my sun-streaked blond hair usually in need of a trim.

It would be one thing if I talked to famous dead people. You know, like that Elvis Presley guy my mother still drools over? I mean, really? The guy would be, like, ancient today! Anyway, if I talked to him, I could give my mom a personal message like, "Sorry we never got to hook up." That would be worth a few extra bucks for allowance, don't you think?

No, the dead people who talk to me are just dead nobodies. Nothing exciting to say. Nothing going down. They're just hanging out, waiting for—I don't know—to be more dead, I guess. Or to see how much trouble they can get me in.

Take today in math class. We're taking this test, see. I'm concentrating real hard on this problem trying to figure height or something. Then I hear this:

"Hey you."

I jerk up in my chair, searching for the guy doing the talking. I glance at the kids on either side of me. Nothing. I look up at the teacher. He's glaring at me.

"Great," I whisper. "He probably thinks I'm trying to cheat." I bow my head and focus on the problem again.

"You, I'm talking to you."

I shake my head in hopes of tossing out that voice. I know now. Some dumb dead guy wants to talk to me.

"Would you be quiet? I'm trying to take a math test."

"Oh sure, that's okay for you to say. I'll never take another test again." His voice breaks up like bad radio reception.

"Not my problem."

"I died too soon, I really did."

"Look, I haven't talked to one yet who didn't say that. Kind of goes with the dead part. Now leave me alone. You're going to make me fail this test."

I hear him snort like he has to blow his nose, if the dead can actually do that. Then comes the kicker.

"I just want another chance. I promise I'll do better."

"I'm going to say this one more time. Not my problem.

Now leave me alone." I form three exclamation points in my head so if he is reading my thoughts as well as listening, he will get the picture.

"But it isn't fair," he whines. *"It just isn't fair."*

Okay. I'm fed up with this guy. I can't even remember the formula for the problem I'm trying to answer. I am definitely going to fail if he keeps on yapping. I try to ignore him and concentrate on remembering the stupid formula.

"Not fair."

My brain is fried, and I've had enough. I slam my pencil on my desk and stand up. "Bud, I don't give a damn if it isn't fair. Just shut the hell up so I can get this test done!"

Did you get the part where I "stand up and yell"? Yep, that earns me an F on the test AND a trip to the AP's office. I can't even defend myself. What am I going to say? "Excuse me, I'm sorry I blurted out loud in the middle of a test, and I'm sorry for cussing, but you see, this dead person wouldn't shut up." Yeah, that would go over well. Nope, I just sit with my head down, my face burning from embarrassment, and whisper, "It won't happen again. Had to be the stress over the test." You get the picture.

The rest of the day I endure the strange looks and whispers by shrugging and mumbling something like "Idiot dead people." The kids will avoid me for the next few days. I think they're afraid whatever I have will rub off on them, or that I've gone bananas or something. Understandable.

All this comes from my grandmother. When I was little, Nana lived with us, and it was like Halloween every night. She told the most amazing stories about spirits that visited her. Nana said I would inherit her gift, except it's not a gift. It is definitely a curse. Because of it, I had the first and last sleepover at my house in the third grade when Nana decided to share one of her stories with my best friend Rachel and me. In the years since Nana passed away, I've been laughed at, shunned, and avoided, especially after an incident like today.

When my parents get home and hear what happened...Well I might be the one shouting "It's not fair."

So now I sit in my bedroom trying to work on a history project. You know, the kind where the teacher puts you in a group, and then no one in the group does anything? Yep, that's my luck. This is due the day after tomorrow, and no one except me has done anything. I'll probably fail if it's not finished. My eyes wander around the room instead of focusing.

"Roosa."

Without thinking, I blurt out, "It's Rosa, not Roosa. And I told you to get lost. Now." I jump to the door and slam it shut. Do the dead have no respect?

And just who is THIS guy? It's not the same person who got me in trouble at school. That's nice. Now I have an army of dead people invading my brain.

Too bad they can't do this project for me.

"Roosa."

Who is this idiot?

"Listen. This is my room, my space. These are my things, and I refuse to share them with dead people!"

I jump on top of my bed; I'm just getting warmed up. It has been a stressful day.

"These are my favorite books on this bookcase. See, my marked up copy of *The Once and Future King.* Here is my *Black Stallion* series. And, here, my Grandpa's <u>National Geographic</u> magazines where I first read about King Tut. All mine!"

I think I'm going nuts. Who rants and raves at the dead? Shaking with frustration, I jump down and sit at my desk. The stupid history project stares back at me. At least it's on ancient Egypt. Something I'm interested in.

"Roosa."

Will this guy never give up?

We're supposed to chronicle the reigns of the 18th Dynasty and evaluate the successes/failures of each pharaoh. I chose King Tutankhamen. Mom took me to the Tut exhibit when it toured the US. Talk about magnificent! I still have my ticket stub pinned on the wall above my desk.

"Roosa."

"I hear nothing."

King Tut ruled Egypt at the age of nine over

three thousand years ago. It wasn't until 1922 that Howard Carter discovered his hidden burial site.

Next to the Tut ticket is my favorite picture of Ankhesenamun and Tut. You know the one: it's on the back of the Golden Throne. He's sitting in the throne; she's standing facing him, one arm outstretched, touching him. I'm not a romantic—well, maybe a little. The point is, in that picture, the love they feel for each other is so obvious. I'm going to use it for the presentation. It's the one item that shows them as real people, not just a part of history.

I like looking at that picture. Sometimes I even imagine myself as Ankhesenamun. I know, I have no life. You try being in tenth grade and living with a curse. See how many boyfriends you have.

Sometimes I think they are discussing their future. You know, how many children they'll have, and how they'll raise them. Maybe they talk about what's happening in Egypt, and she shows her support with a simple touch on his arm. They could also be talking about where they'll be buried. They did that, you know. Had their burial chambers ready years before their deaths.

On days like today when I'm feeling depressed—the curse will do that to me—it could be Ankhesenamun is saying goodbye to Tut as he dies. She assures him they will meet in the afterlife. What would it be like to wander the earth looking for my husband's spirit or *ba*? Does Tut look for hers?

"I do, Roosa."

I turn around and scream.

Chapter 2

OMG. Standing in my bedroom is the most gorgeous guy I have ever seen. He could be an upperclassman at school.

His head is bald; shaved is in these days, you know. His nose is so cute! He's tanned and so buff all over. Oh yeah, I could fall for him, except he's wearing a sleeveless t-shirt and something that looks like a skort! Where did he come from?

Wait a minute. He called me Roosa. I hear his voice, and it's not in my head!

I scramble out of my chair and back up against the wall.

"Who are you?" I know, but there is just no way.

"You know who I am, Roosa."

I just stare, blink, and stare some more.

"No way." I shake my head vigorously. "I hear you guys, but no one, I mean no one, ever shows himself."

"I'm sorry to frighten you. It is not my reason for coming here."

"Really? Really? You didn't want to frighten me?" My voice starts rising along with my anger. "Well, let me tell you, you...mister, whoever you are, you did frighten me. In fact, you're scaring the heck out of me. Just how did you get into this house? You need to leave before I call the police."

I take a shaky breath and press harder against the wall.

What am I going to tell the police? Excuse me, but I would like to report an uninvited ghost in my bedroom. That's sure to get me put in the looney bin. No way can I explain who I'm talking to, and God forbid if this ..., this hunk, can be seen by others. The girls in my classes would run over themselves to get his attention. And me, my parents will ground me for the rest of my life for being at home alone with a complete stranger, not to mention a boy.

I decide to try a less hysterical approach.

"Okay, you've had your fun. Now you need to leave before my parents get home. I can't begin to explain your presence in my bedroom. I don't even care who you are, you just need to leave, *please*." I put special emphasis on the please, just hoping that my brain will respond to my desperate plea and make this...this whatever, disappear.

"I take my leave, Roosa, but not without you. I need you."

What? Okay, take a deep breath, girl. A boy you don't even know appears in your bedroom and says that he needs you. You, who talks to the dead, who can't even get a date to the fall dance two weeks from now.

What is happening to me? I have to get rid of him, real or not, right?

"Why do you need me?" Wait a minute, what am I doing? This is not getting rid of him.

"Do you know who I am, Roosa?"

Is it just me, or can you feel how the way he says my name sends shivers down my back?

"I know who I think you are, but that's nuts. Impossible."

"I have found that nothing is impossible when souls are involved. We are all connected, some just more than others. Nothing prevents us from moving through time. You, unlike most, are able to connect with spirits inhabiting the afterlife. Yours speaks to us. It is strong, Roosa, and I have need of your strength."

There are those words again. *He needs me.*

Get hold of yourself, Rosa. This is some whack-job who has managed to get into your house and is probably getting ready to rape or kill you. You need to scream, run, do anything except stand there and drool. This is not who you think it is. It's impossible. Impossible, do you hear?

Yeah, I hear.

"Are you really Tutankhamen?"

Chapter 3

"Yes."

That's all he says? 'Yes'? Don't you think that if some gorgeous dude, even if he is over three thousand years old, shows up in your bedroom you would expect him to say more? I mean, come on.

"That's all you have to say? How do I even know that you're real and not just someone my crazy brain has made up?"

"Touch me, Roosa. You will see I'm real enough."

Touch him? Is he as crazy as I am? Okay, so I'm going to touch him, just for my own peace of mind.

I reach out my hand, fingers extended, trying to reach him but not move from the wall. A crooked smile appears on his face. He takes a couple of steps forward, reaches out and touches me.

Lightning heat shoots out from him, races up my arm, switches direction and dives into my stomach. I snatch my hand back and grab my belly with both hands. The burning sensation knocks my knees out from under me. I slump to the floor, still leaning on the wall. The room spins, and my head swims. Tears mixed with stars blur my vision so there is no focusing. Not enough air in here; my chest tightens as if the lungs inside are ready to explode.

The burning sensation turns into a glow. My whole body's glowing! Blinking, I concentrate on the hand in front of me. Glowing, definitely glowing! Crazy. I have finally gone over the edge. I'm going crazy fast, and no one is home to save me.

Tut's eyes are a tangible weight as he stares at me. He stands there, not saying a word, his crooked smile replaced by tenderness, hope, concern? I rub my temples to ease the pounding pain that is suddenly present. Fear leaps through me like wildfire through dry grass. What is happening?

"I won't hurt you, Rosa."

What? A girl's voice! I look around the room. No one else is here. I look at Tut; his eyes lock with mine. What is going on? I joke a lot about my gift being a curse, but this time I'm really afraid. Like the afraid of dying kind of fear.

And Tut, he looks like he's seen a ghost, except in this case, like he's heard a ghost.

Oh, please don't let me be crazy. His form fades right in front of me turning translucent. Hot flashes rock my body. Icy shivers grip me. I think I'm going to faint.

"Rosa, it's all right."

The fervid heat and biting cold leave me. My eyesight sharpens.

"Let me out. Let me just look on him for a moment. Please, I don't have much time."

How do I respond to a request like that? I clutch at my aching stomach; it's as if I haven't eaten in days and it's demanding food right now. Is the weird girl voice doing this to me? I can't keep control. Horrible empty feelings of longing wash over me. I let them carry me away.

All of a sudden Tut's eyes change. If it's possible, they soften. I know, you think I'm really crazy, don't you? Well, you're not alone.

As he reaches out again, my body moves without my consent. Skin connects with skin, and this time the glow envelopes both of us. No burning, just glow. Slowly, he covers my fingers with his.

Never have I ever felt anything so, so, I don't know. My flesh melts into his like cheese on toasted bread. Pretty dumb, huh?

He sighs.

Then so quietly I barely hear, he utters, "Ankhesenamun."

Chapter 4

"**R**oosa."

I struggle to open my eyes. Where am I? Home? Did I faint? Oh, my aching head.

"Roosa. Wake up. Time is fleeing."

That gets through. I mean, who says 'time is fleeing'? Time is not alive. More important, am I alive? Am I still glowing?

"Roosa." More urgently this time.

My eyes open. He's still here, kneeling beside my bed, his bronze hand gently but firmly patting mine.

"You are awake. Good. We must prepare to leave at once."

Whoa there. Is this guy crazy as well as good-looking? What's he talking about?

"I'm not going anywhere," I say as I sit up. *Particularly with a ghost.*

"But you must. You are my only hope."

No one has ever said that to me before. This may have possibilities.

"What are you talking about?"

"She lives within you. A piece of her *ba* lives within you."

"You mean Ankhesenamun?"

"Yes."

Love those one word answers, but I know he's right. I remember the spark that passed between us. It still echoes inside me. That should be impossible, shouldn't it?

"I see you doubt my words. You felt her. When we touched, she ignited inside of you. It is you I have been searching for. You are the one who can lead me to Ankhesenamun's final resting place. Only you."

A part of Ankhesenamun lives in me? Spirits can't live inside real people, can they? I don't know how and don't want to know. I just don't want to experience that again.

"This is insane. Even if I did believe you—me—her." I shake my head. "I can't help you find her. She's been dead for nearly thirty-four-hundred years."

"So have I, but I found you." He steps closer. "You have her eyes, Roosa. Those green orbs that emeralds get lost in."

Okay, so now what, Rosa?

Tut moves back, and takes a deep breath. "Roosa, I only have seven days to find Ay and perform the Opening of the Mouth ceremony to learn where he laid Ankhesenamun to rest. We have to hurry. We must go now."

This is not a boy before me speaking now. This voice is unaccustomed to being told no. This is the voice of a leader, a ruler, a pharaoh. This is King Tutankhamen speaking.

"I don't understand any of this. Where do you think I'm going to go with you? Who is Ay? What is this opening mouth bit?"

I actually do know some of the answers. Ay was Ankhesenamun's grandfather although for some reason she called him uncle. He succeeded Tut on the throne of Egypt. I've even heard of the ceremony of Opening of the Mouth. What I don't know is what this has to do with me.

His sigh fills the room—angry, frustrated, and weary.

"Roosa, I need to find Ay before General Horemheb erases his existence forever. Ay is the only one who knows where Ankhesenamun's tomb is located. He arranged for her burial. If in seven days, when the flooding of the Nile has reached Memphis, I haven't located Ay and Ankhesenamun, Horemheb will acknowledge his son as his successor, and his line will continue in honor," he paused. "And my family will forever be seen as traitors to Egypt. We will vanish from history."

"I don't understand. You're in our history books. You're my project!" I point to my desk. "People stood in line to see the artifacts found in your tomb. I stood in line! The only pharaoh people didn't like was

Akhenaten because he dumped the old gods for a new one."

"He is my father, Roosa."

"Oh." I knew that. "But you're not like him. You brought back the old gods. You saved Egypt. He's the one seen as a traitor, not you."

"My father was *not* a traitor. He did nothing other pharaohs before him hadn't done."

"But he forbade the worship of the Amun god. He left Thebes and closed the temples. He built his own city and worshipped that, that Aten god. He made the people follow him or be put to death."

"No! That's Horemheb's lies. That's what he did. Made the Egyptians discredit us all because he was angry. Angry that I was my father's successor and not him. Angry that Ay kept the news of my death from him so that Ay would succeed me as pharaoh. He married Nefertiti's sister just to be pharaoh."

"But what about the Aten? Your father did worship the sun disk, not Re the sun god."

"All pharaohs worshipped their favorite god in their temples."

"What about the Amun temples, the Amun priests?"

"My father needed money to build his city. He and Nefertiti felt exposed in Thebes. They wanted to raise their family away from that danger. The money he took from the temples belonged to him as pharaoh. The priests had become greedy; they closed the temples in an attempt to fuel the people's anger against him. The only wrong decision my father made was to pull Egypt's troops from her borders to build his city."

"Horemheb was a general," I added. "He felt he couldn't defend his country."

Tut nodded. "I sent the troops back after I became pharaoh. Ankhesenamun and I moved to Thebes away from the sad memories. We do not deserve to be called traitors. But it is more than just setting the record straight, saving my family's place in history."

He pauses and picks up my hand again. There is no spark this time. Longing and sadness fill his ebony eyes.

"I will lose Ankhesenamun forever." His chin lowers to his bare chest.

Through our linked hands, the shudders that envelope his body threaten to overflow into mine. I look at the picture of him and Ankhesenamun by the desk and make up my mind. This time, the spirit inside me reaches out to the young pharaoh seated on the throne. I remove my hand and touch him on the arm as she does in the picture. He raises his head and those eyes look deep into mine, questioning.

"I will help you find Ankhesenamun," I whisper.

Chapter 5

His hand covers mine, brings it to his lips. There is no painful spark this time. This spark feels...wonderful.

"Thank you, Roosa."

"Do you think that you could get my name right? It's Rosa. Say that."

"Roosa."

He smiles, not understanding what I mean.

Standing, he pulls me up beside him. "We must leave now. There is no time to get lost."

"To lose."

He arches his eyebrow.

I shake my head and roll my eyes. This is going to take getting used to. "Where are we going and for how long? My parents are out with friends for dinner and a movie. They won't be coming home until midnight."

"What is this movie?"

"Never mind, it would take too long to explain. Where are we off to?"

"We must travel back to the Egypt of my time. There we must try to waken more of Ankhesenamun and find Ay. "

I stop listening almost as soon as he starts talking. The Egypt of his time? Ancient Egypt? Visions of the pyramids, the Sphinx, the ancient temples, and the Nile flash through my brain. What a trip that would be!

Wait a minute, sister. You don't have time to go to the Egypt of today and be home before your parents get back. And he wants you to go back to ancient Egypt!

"Wait. Just wait a darn minute," I say to myself and Tut. "I just told you that my parents would be back at midnight. I have to, must be here, by then. I'm not going to ancient Egypt."

"No, Roosa. You do not understand." He steps forward, and I step back.

"It's you who doesn't understand. I thought you meant we were going to, going to...I don't know what I thought." It would be something to tell my, my...Right, I could tell the kids in my classes that I went to ancient Egypt with the ghost of King Tut. Can you hear the death knell? Bring out the strait jacket. "I can't help you."

"There is no one else who can, Roosa." I start to interrupt him. "No, wait. Listen. Going back to ancient Egypt is the only way. We must retrace the steps of our lives. We must search for clues that will tell us where to find Ay. The answer is there, somewhere, in the past we shared: me, Ankhesenamun, Ay, and General Horemheb."

I start to protest again.

His finger silences my lips.

"It will not be as you think. I have traveled here from my Egypt. As I have been here with you, Re is now completing his journey across the sky. Soon he will disappear into the Duat to surface again tomorrow. Then we will have only six days left."

"I don't understand." I run my fingertips through my hair.

"Stay here," he says. "I will return when Re is ready to begin the next day. Then you will understand."

With that, he leaves. I mean he really leaves. Disappears without a trace. Tentatively I move forward, standing where he stood. Nothing.

There's a tap on my shoulder and then the now familiar "Roosa."

I jump straight up, sure that I've left my clothes on the floor. Turning, I stare at him.

"How? What? How?"

"Day is getting ready to break. Re is on the move. We have only six days left."

"How could that be? You just left."

"It is as I told you. Only minutes will pass in your world when you are in mine. You will be home before your parents arrive unless Horemheb catches us in one of his traps."

"But how?"

"We travel on what is known as a time wrap. Time wraps around and around. We are able to move across eons that way. In your world, the days pass as normal. In my Egypt, they go by much faster although one does not know that when there. It is only when moving into another time that one notices the differences. That is all I can tell you."

"Time wrap, huh? Sounds like somebody's idea for the next superhero movie." I pause, knowing that I might regret my next words, but one look at Ankhesenamun's arm on his leaves no doubt that I'm already in up to my neck. "Okay, show me how to use this time wrap."

He pulls me close. Moisture from the Nile on his skin assails my senses and the heat of the desert sun warms my body where he touches me. What if I don't want to come home? What if I just stay? No dance, no grounding, no worries. Just him and me. Wait. Did he say something about traps?

"Hey! What about General Horemheb? What traps?" My head starts spinning and stars zip across my eyes.

Chapter 6

Not spinning; no stars. Well, at least that's over. Can't say that my stomach cares. It's still sloshing around. Ugh! Waves of nausea and cold sweat keep coming. Maybe this wasn't such a good idea.

"Roosa."

I try a couple of times to focus my eyes. OMG the sun is hot.

"Roosa."

"Okay, okay. Give me a minute."

My eyes open one at time. The sun burns like I am sitting on top of it. Shading my face, I look around. We're in the middle of a city, but no city that I've ever been in. Some people are dressed similar to Tut, but there are also people in long white gowns. Women balancing baskets on their heads filled with goods walk by, their bodies relaxed in spite of the heavy load they are carrying. They don't look down but tread confidently along on ground worn smooth by the passage of many feet.

I step back as a line of donkeys and water buffalo approach from the opposite direction. Dark-skinned men lead the animals loaded with wheat, reeds, vegetables and fruits in carriers in the opposite direction of the women. The smell of crushed produce hangs in the air as they file by. Weaving through the crowded street, small children, dressed in short tunics, clamber to pick up the fallen fruit before it is stepped on by beasts and man. Their laughter echoes throughout the street and mixes in with the chatter of strange sounds as the adults twist and bend to avoid them.

So out of my element here. So very glad of the small wall between me and this Egypt. Granted, the wall is only two rows of handmade bricks that mark the edge of the road on either side, but hey, it's better than nothing. Small stones imbedded in the ground make walkways on each side.

"Where are we?"

"In my Egypt," he answers. A smile lights up his face as he surveys the city in front of us. "The city of my youth, Akhet-Aten. This is where Ankhesenamun and I spent our childhood and part of our married life."

I look again at the surge of life around me. Ancient Egypt. Wish I had my phone with me, the pictures I could bring back. Surveying the scene, the beauty of his city amazes me. It bustles with the everyday activities of the people. The essence of this long forgotten culture seems to battle the searing sun for recognition, prominence, and survival. Large brick walls, similar to the fences at home, run along the pathway as far as I can see. The heat reflects off those white blocks creating a torrid inferno. My throat burns even as I take shallow breaths to avoid scalding my lungs. In the distance an obelisk stretches up to the heavens, dwarfing everything around it just as Washington's monument does. Its shadow casts a long line over the city even as the sun reflecting off it intensifies the heat. I wonder if it marks a temple or the palace of Tut's father? My wonderings end when Tut strides off in that direction.

My attempts to catch up with him are waylaid by the heat and curiosity. I pause with each step to breathe in this exotic atmosphere. Here and there small stands of trees—oases really—off to the side provide some relief from the sun. Might be nice to stop. How people live in this oven is beyond me. Even the sweat pouring down my back is hot. So much for the premise that a person's body perspiring cools them off. I keep wiping the stinging saltwater from my eyes. My feet slide in my soggy shoes making it hard to walk. Be lucky if I don't have blisters. Never knew a person had this much water in them.

Hieroglyphs decorate the white walls beside us. I recognize a couple, the Eye of Horus and the Ankh; maybe the rest indicate who lives or works there.

"Tut? What does this say?" I point to one set of

hieroglyphs.

Moving closer, he studies the symbols. "The family is asking for Horus to watch over them and their child. There is some sickness afflicting the child. They also ask for the Aten to protect and provide a long life for the child."

"The Aten? Which is that?"

He points to a small rounded disk above the carving of a child. Coming out of all sides are rays. I remember drawing a similar sun when I was small. At the end of each of these rays, however, tiny hands stretch out toward the child. I wonder if the child got better? As soon as the thought passes, I get a brain freeze. I'm here in Egypt, but not the Egypt of my day. I'm in a country no one has ever seen, no one alive that is. The overwhelming power of that thought weakens my knees, and I collapse.

"Roosa, are you all right?"

He sounds genuinely concerned, and I'm grateful. I'm not sure how I'm going to deal with all this.

"I think so. It's just so much more than I ever thought. All the buildings. The people. Nothing of this remains in my world."

"We are not here to look at the sights."

I hear the impatience in his voice.

"We must find Ay. Come, Roosa. I will take you back to when I was five, and my father first acknowledged me as his son."

"You're kidding, right? What kind of a father doesn't even admit that you are his son? Five years old, really?"

"No. You forget this is Egypt three thousand years ago. The death rate among our children is high. Many do not live to even be five. Some do not survive birth." His voice breaks, and the great sadness behind his words threatens to overwhelm me. I want to ask him what is wrong, but a tiny voice inside says not to ask this. It will break his heart again.

I look up at him puzzled, but the moment is gone. He takes my arm and starts walking toward what I guess might be the palace. The closer we get, the taller the columns rise, almost touching the sky. I stretch to see the tops of them, but he pulls me with him.

"Come now. She is on her way to my room. This way." He disappears to the right as we cross between the largest doors I have ever seen. Each door contains half of the Aten made from gold, with jewels I recognize as blue faience from the Tut exhibit, outlining the gold. I try to stop and touch the design, but Tut tugs me away.

"Here." He stops.

We stand in a hall with its walls literally flowering with blossoms from the Nile. Some are carved into the plaster; others are placed in delicately designed vases. Blues, reds, yellows, oranges, and purples. It's like stepping out into a spring garden.

"We wait. She will come."

"Who?"

"Ankhesenamun," he whispers.

At that moment a young girl comes running around a corner. Her long black hair trails behind. She appears older than six by a couple of years, but it's hard to tell. The black kohl around her eyes ages her as does the makeup she wears. She looks older but almost perfect. In my world she could be a child model.

Geez, what I wouldn't give to be able to look like that. Fat chance, though. My mother would haul me into the bathroom and scrub my face until the skin started to fall off if I came home looking like that. And that doesn't even take into account what my father would do.

She wears a simple, white shift decorated with…Wait a minute! That looks like real gold. There is no way a girl this young is wearing real gold. I turn to ask, but one look at the joy on Tut's face hushes my question.

"Tut Khan, Tut Khan, you must get up!"

A boy, even younger than Ankhesenamun opens the door, struggling with the weight. "What is it, Hesena?"

"It is an elephant! One of the generals brought it this morning as a gift for father."

"An elephant? Wherever did he find one?"

"I don't know. Come quickly or we'll miss it!"

She whirls around and runs down the hallway.

Then as quickly as she came, they both disappear.

"Your father got elephants for gifts?" I can't believe what I heard. An elephant, an elephant? All I got for my last birthday was a blue sweater, a couple of books, and some gift cards.

"Yes, an elephant. You see, Roosa, this day is to be one of great importance for me. I just didn't know it then." He pauses. "Come, let's go to the throne room. It's where they are going."

We follow in the footsteps of the past. Tut hurries, impatience sitting as a frown upon his face as I lag behind. I come to a stop at the doors of the throne room. The arched entrance is lined with carvings and paintings of the Aten, the tiny hands at the ends of the rays reaching out for me. Tut glares at me as he shoves me through the doors.

In front of us stands the biggest animal I have ever seen. I've seen elephants in the zoo, who hasn't? But this isn't behind a fence. This elephant is only a few feet in front of me. It is beautiful. With a couple of steps I could actually touch it. Unconsciously my arm reaches out.

"No, Roosa," Tut said. "We must not break the time wrap. We cannot interfere or touch or talk to anyone here. To do so would create a ripple that could destroy time and leave us trapped here forever."

Reluctantly I lower my arm, but not my eyes. It's such a magnificent creature. It stands there, the smooth gray skin dripping water. The enormous legs and feet shift nonstop in agitation. Ears as big as me flap nervously as its head, too small in proportion to its body, swings back and forth. Its tiny eyes seem to be seeking a way out. A long trunk framed by gigantic tusks extends from the front of the head.

Suddenly, the trunk arches and stretches upward. The blast of noise threatens to deafen all in the room. I watch as Hesena and the other Tut clap their hands over their ears. We do the same.

A tall man stands and motions at the door. His lips are moving, but I can't hear a word. A cone-shaped hat sits on his head and a kilt-like garment swishes against his legs. Light sparkles off the huge jeweled necklace that rests on his bare chest. It appears to sway as he breathes. Good thing the necklace is pretty because he is ugly. Oops, I'm not supposed to say that. But talk about an unattractive man. It's his nose—so square and large—that really makes him that way.

Sitting next to him is the most beautiful woman I've ever seen. Black hair frames her delicate face, an older version of Ankhesenamun's, and earrings shaped as gold eyes dangle from her tiny ears. Her bare shoulders sparkle like glitter above a golden gown that flows down her slender body. It is gathered at the waist with a jewel-encrusted belt. She looks stunning and totally unaffected by the huge elephant.

"Who are those two?" I ask, nodding my head in

their direction. Tut averts his eyes from the scene in front of us.

"That is my father, Akhenaten."

"Oh." I can't seem to manage any more than that. They don't really look like father and son, but then I don't see the resemblance between my dad and me. My grandmother always said I favored him.

"And that is his wife and Hesena's mother, Nefertiti."

Well, you could knock me over with a feather. This is the most talked about queen in all of Egyptian history. Everything I've read says that her beauty knows no comparison. The evidence stands right here in front of me.

I look back to Tut's father. How in the world does someone that beautiful marry someone like that?

A man, who I didn't see before, appears from the other side of the animal. He's dressed in a white gown like those people in the movies who live in the desert. He touches the gray beast on the left side. The animal ceases its trumpeting, turns, and follows the man out the door.

Tut jabs me with his elbow. "I remember thinking how funny that tail was," he says. He chuckles softly. "If the head of this animal is too small for the enormous body, then the tail is woefully out of place. It is too short to be of any use flicking away flies and gnats and couldn't even reach halfway up the body."

I watch as Akhenaten holds out his hand to the

boy Tut. Hesena pushes him forward. The young Tut hesitates, and his small hand is swallowed up in the larger one. A smile, ever so slight, breaks the plane of the older man's face and softens its harsh look.

I look questioningly at Tut. A grin spreads across his entire face. I put my hand on his arm and feel his pulse racing.

He turns at my touch. "That was the first time my father acknowledged that I was his son, his heir. It was a monumental time for me and all of Egypt, Roosa. It should have been a time filled with joy, but instead, it solidified Nefertiti's hatred of me. She loathed the fact a bastard was being acknowledged as the next pharaoh of Egypt instead of their eldest daughter Meritaten."

I'm having trouble taking all this in. Akhenaten, Nefertiti, Tut, Hesena—and me—all in the same room, well sort of anyway. I'm beginning to wonder where I'm headed and how I'm going to get home. Nerves make my stomach flip uneasily.

Chills come over me like my blood is made up of ice water running throughout my body. I shiver. I try to shrink behind Tut. *Evil.* I remember how my grandmother would describe these feelings. Rosa, she would say. It feels like someone is walking over my grave. I would look at her, not understanding. She wasn't dead. How in the world could someone walk over her grave? I know now. And whoever is doing the walking leaves evil in each of his footprints.

The king and the other Tut follow the elephant out a side door, and Hesena trails behind.

Nefertiti walks by, elegant and regal. Her imperial gaze halts any who might think to precede her. One by one, the people stand aside and bow their heads as she floats past. Her gaze sweeps over us, but it is not evil, just interested, as if she senses something where we stand.

"She can't see us, can she?"

"No, Roosa. My people cannot see us. It is not allowed. Come, let's follow," he says. "I want to show you my father's zoo."

"Your father has a zoo! No way. No one owns a zoo, no..." I stop short. Tut's image wavers before me. I suck in air, but my lungs feel empty. Pulsing blood thunders through my body. My fingers turn white at the knuckles as I clutch his hand. It's as if I've just been punched in the stomach. Evil envelopes me, threatening to squeeze the life out of me. Please body, breathe! Am I dying? How can this be? No one can see us!

Tut whirls around. He must feel it also.

There in a corner of the room, behind the double throne is a man, but not a man. I can see right through him.

"It is Horemheb. Or rather Horemheb's *ba*. It is not allowed here. Not here with us, now. This is my home, my time." Tut draws in a sharp breath. He starts toward the *ba* or ghost or whatever, but it is gone.

The invisible grip on my throat tightens even more, then the aura of evil lifts. I can breathe easy once more, and the blood no longer barrels through me like an avalanche of snow on a deep slope.

Tut whispers. "We must find somewhere to hide. Someplace where we will be safe for a while. It is not safe here." He caresses my cheek, tracing my jaw with his finger.

I draw in a quick breath, and my eyes flutter closed. A voice speaks inside of me. It is Hesena.

"You must do as Tut Khan asks. General Horemheb's ba is dangerous. Just now he could have killed you, us. Don't question, just follow Tut Khan."

My lids raise and I stare into Tut's black eyes.

"It is as she says, Roosa. Come. We are in danger the longer we stay here." He leads me under the golden archway with the huge doors we entered earlier.

I follow him, not knowing what else to do.

I know what she told me is true. I felt it throughout my entire being. He possessed enough power to kill me right there. What have I done? What if I die here? What if I can't go home again?

Chapter 7

Passing through the doors, Tut turns right, not left which was the way we came in. The only sound comes from our shoes on the polished granite floor squeaking like basketball shoes on a gym floor. We meet no one. The walls we pass repeat the signs of the Aten and the Ankh. The god and life. No illumination, no windows, only the occasional light from the skylights above.

Tut hasn't spoken since we left the throne room. Time to find out what is happening. "Tut?"

"Yes?" He doesn't stop, but continues on.

"Tut?" I repeat. This time I reach out and touch his arm from behind.

He turns and those dark eyes hold annoyance at being questioned.

"What, Roosa?"

"Where are we going? Will Horemheb be able to follow? What happened back there? How could he see us?"

Tut holds up his hand. "Not yet. I will try to answer your questions once we are beyond all ears." He walks on.

Okay, I guess. There still isn't a sign of anyone near us. In fact, the silence of the hall is more disconcerting than calming. I follow. What else am I going to do?

Several minutes pass before Tut reaches a wooden door, a locked wooden door. It reminds me of the doors I've read about in fantasy stories, dungeon doors built of oak and nearly five inches thick, heavy, and immovable. I wonder what's beyond? Not a dungeon, I hope.

He pushes on the wall above the door. An opening the size of a fist appears. Tut reaches in and takes an object out. It is a key shaped like the ankh and made of what looks like granite.

"Been here before, huh?"

Tut gives me one of those looks. You know, one that says 'Did you really say that?' I shrug and give him a weak grin.

Sliding the key into the lock, Tut turns it. In the silence, the movement of the device screams. I look behind me. What if someone has heard?

The door opens easily. Tut motions me in. For a second I wonder if this is the end. If I have been brought all this way to die to appease Horemheb. Then I remember her, the one inside me. I walk through and into another long hallway.

Tut closes and locks the door, keeping the key. At my questioning look, he says, "As long as I have the key, no one can enter here. I'll put it back later."

"What about the other end?" The hall stretches beyond us lighted as before by skylights. Here the air is cooler, although the sun's rays add warmth to the cold granite.

"No one will approach from that way. The door is barred from the inside. Come, up ahead is a place we can talk."

The hall slopes upward toward brighter sunlight. A huge skylight or maybe a window. That would be nice, a window that is. I have no idea where we are in relation to where we first entered the palace. I'm guessing we are still in the building somewhere, but I'm not even sure of that.

Tut steps into the sunlight. My breath catches in my throat. The light bathes him in a nimbus of gold. Surrounded by the sun's rays, he appears taller and more like the spirit he is. I struggle not to fall on my knees before him. Where are we?

The corners of his mouth turn up just a bit, softening his features as he holds out his hand. Unsure, I hesitate. He reaches down, takes my hand, and pulls me next to him. The glow threatens to blind me. Covering my eyes, I peek through my fingers while my eyes adjust to the brightness.

Tut is standing by a window situated in a small alcove. Above a skylight lets the sun shine in, and its rays bounce off walls of gold. Really? Walls of gold? I reach out and touch the brilliant wall warmed by the sun. It is gold, and its surface warms my hands, almost burning them.

"This is real gold."

"Yes."

There's that one-word response again. It's frustrating.

"What is this place?"

"This is the Window of Appearances." He points out the window. "Down there the people of Akhet-Aten would gather. Here is where my father and Nefertiti would be standing, like gods looking down on them. That is why all the gold. It reflects the golden light from the sun onto them. Our people believed that the pharaohs were the embodiment of the gods. This re-enforced that belief."

Stepping up to the window, I look out as Akhenaten and Nefertiti must have done so long ago. With the golden beams of pure light upon me, I almost feel the power coursing through my body. What power they must have felt.

Tut continues. "From here they bestowed jewels and sacred necklaces on those who had pleased them. Small tokens from the gods. I came sometimes with them. I was not allowed to be seen from the Window, but I could hear the murmur from the crowds as the time drew near for the presentations. The cheers rising from below were deafening when my father and

Nefertiti handed out the rewards."

"Handed out?" I look down. Below the window is a wooden platform.

"Yes. The recipients climbed up like they were ascending stairs to Nut, the sky goddess. Once again, it gave the appearance of receiving gifts from the gods."

I stand for a while longer gazing down, wondering what it would be like to have that much power, to feel that powerful. It is beyond my comprehension.

"I will try to answer your questions, Roosa, but I'm not sure I can," Tut says as he stands next to me. "We are going beyond the other door, to a place of refuge I used as a boy. We must have time to think and plan. We cannot do that here or anywhere else in the palace. Also, Horemheb will not be able to follow us. He did not know of this place I speak of. We will be safe."

I nod and wait for him to continue.

"As to what happened back in the throne room, I have given much thought. Horemheb should not have seen us, should not have been able to harm you." He shakes his head, his face straining under the pressure. "Somehow he has grasped the dark magic of the gods, magic that demands sacrifice. I fear he has traded his life, maybe even his soul for this magic. We must be careful. As we have seen, this magic travels through time." He pauses. "I am sorry, Roosa. I did not know of this before now. I fear I have put you in danger."

I sit in silence, digesting his words. Danger, but also an excitement I try to deny but can't. Where will it lead me, I wonder? I dare not think too long on this or I may lose my strength. "Let's go to that refuge. I think the further away we are from here, the better it will be."

He nods and leaves the window. I look one last time, imaging the people cheering, applauding me before I turn and follow him.

Reaching the other door, wooden and imposing as its twin, Tut unbars it. We continue down a tunnel on a dirt path to a room so close to the Nile that I can hear the waters rushing by. In places the river has seeped in swallowing part of the floor. The shadowy wall in front of us shelters a dim opening. Going forward, we climb down to another tunnel and wade a short distance through muddy shallow waters to a small barren room. Here there is a place to sit. I'm still cold and not just from the water we waded through.

Tut has left me here and gone back to replace the key. Opposite me, another pathway leads outside. The shivering won't stop, but the cold isn't the only reason for my shaking. Not only am I cursed because I can talk to the dead, but now I travel with them and see others. Not to mention that one of them could have killed me if he wished. I don't know about anybody else, but I certainly didn't come here to die. No way. No how.

Tut's been gone a long time. I wish he'd hurry back. Geez, I think I just want to go home where people don't try to strangle you. Where is he?

"Right behind you, Roosa."

"Can't you knock or something? Do you have to always sneak up on me?"

"I am sorry. Look, I brought some water." He holds out a plain earthen jug. Like a prisoner on his last day, I grab the water and chug until I choke. Then remembering my manners, I hand the jug to Tut and lean back against the cool stone. Tut sits opposite me.

For a few moments, neither of us speak. I don't know about him, but it was like I hadn't had a drink in days. Must be the heat and the fear.

"Look, Tut," I say. "I know that I said I would help you, but I just want to go home. I want you to take me home."

He says nothing, just stares at me with this sad look on his face.

"I know that you are afraid. For that I am sorry. As for General Horemheb..."

"I want to forget General Horemheb and everything about this place. I want to go home, Tut. Now. I don't like it here."

His fingers touch my cheek. Gentle shockwaves shoot down my body. I look at him, not sure why he is doing this. I start to ask, but the words do not come. Instead I hear her.

"Rosa, please. Tut Khan and I need you. The piece of me

that lives within you is fading. If we cannot find Ay's ba, then all will be lost. I will be lost forever. Tut Khan and I will never be together in the afterlife."

Her words leave me with none of my own.

"Rosa, have you ever been in love?"

Out loud I answer her, embarrassed. "No."

"Someday you will be, and it will be the most wonderful thing. But for now, please understand. Tut Khan and I were only together nine short years. We pledged to stay together for all eternity. General Horemheb will deny us that and condemn Tut Khan, my father, Akhenaten, Ay, and even myself as traitors to all of Egypt."

"Why can't you just use me to tell Tut where your burial chamber is?"

"Because the part of my ba talking to you does not know."

"Wait just a minute. How can you not know? You are her."

"Not really. I mean I am, but I'm not."

Okay, does that sound crazy just to me?

"When General Horemheb denied Ay the Opening of the Mouth, not only was the location of my burial chamber lost, but my ba was separated from my ka or spiritual body. And in that separation, my knowledge of Hesena's resting place was lost also."

I say nothing. I just try to take this all in. Spirits, bodies, separation, loss. Geez, I thought my world was complicated. Smack me if I ever complain again.

"Please, Rosa. Tut Khan can protect you. We need you."

The voice goes silent. The shock waves stop. Tut stands there, his ebony eyes burning into mine. He knows I've talked to her. He could hear me, but not her.

Without a word uttered, I sense Tut's plea. I remember back in my bedroom—boy, that seems like ages ago—I gave my word.

But then you didn't know that some ghost, *ba*, whatever, had plans to kill you, my brain yells.

I know, but when Tut touches me, the electricity shoots through my veins, not just as her, but as me. Here I am fifteen years old. Most girls I know have had at least one boyfriend and have even gone on dates, even if it was with a group of kids. Me, the last time I held hands with a boy was in the fourth grade. We went on a trip to the zoo, and I had to hold hands with red-headed Erik as we crossed the road. It took me weeks to get the nerve to ask Caleb to the fall dance, and then he said no. How sad is that?

What if the closest I ever get to the love that Ankhesenamun is talking about is right here and now? My heart races when Tut smiles at me. I know he's only seeing her. I mean I'm not that stupid. But I can pretend.

And if I don't help them, there is no one else. Their spirits will be separated for eternity. That's a long time. If I don't help, then somehow they will be wiped from the pages of history. It will be like their love for each other never was. I told you I was a romantic.

     If I never have someone love me like Tut does Hesena, then at least I'll have felt what she felt and know that for myself. And if Tut can't protect me...oh please don't let it come to that. I have to help them.

     "Okay, what do we do next?"

Chapter 8

It's early afternoon and the heat is radiating through the rock. I don't know if it can get hotter. For the last hour or so, we have sat here brainstorming about what to do next. I've asked about General Horemheb and Ay, but Tut hasn't given me a lot of information. I gather that the general disliked Akhenaten and that is what's at the root of all this mess. Ay, Ankhesenamun's grandfather, tried to preserve the honor of Akhenaten, Nefertiti, and Tut, and that is why Horemheb refused the Opening of the Mouth upon Ay's death.

I don't understand all of this.

"Tut?"

He turns from the doorway and cocks his bald head my way.

"We are at an impasse, as they say in my world."

"Impasse?"

"We don't know where to go next, or what to do next. And time is not on our side. I think you need to tell me how this all started. Why General Horemheb dislikes your family so much."

"Dislike is not strong enough, Roosa. He would see us wiped from the history of Egypt."

"I know, but I need to know why. It might be that the clue to Ay's tomb might be in the story."

"You may be right." He sits down, his back against the warm stone. "We have to be on the move again as soon as the heat lessens. It will pass the time and may provide an answer. Come and listen to a story that amazed me as a young boy and will astound you."

Intrigued, I lean forward, elbows on my knees, chin resting on my hands. He could write a book with that hook.

"My father was not a popular leader in his time. People blamed him for everything that went wrong. Rumors spread throughout Egypt that he had cursed his people by abandoning their gods in favor of the Aten, the disk of the sun. Forsaking the other gods upset the Maat, the order of his people's lives.

"As I already told you, my father was not happy in Thebes. He and Nefertiti both feared the city. Once here, he changed his name from Amenhotep to Akhenaten in honor of his god. He even named me Tutankhaten.

"One day after he acknowledged me as his son and heir, my father took me aside and explained some of what was happening. I must have been all of six years old, but I remember our entire conversation."

"Wow," is all that I can say.

"There will come a time, son, when your turn to rule Egypt is at hand," he said. "You need to understand why I embrace the god Aten, but also that I have not abandoned all the other gods."

"I am listening my Royal Father."

"And so he began a story about the mighty Sphinx of Giza so fascinating that when I visited there I hoped to hear the Sphinx speak to me as it once did to my great-grandfather Tuthmosis IV, son of the Pharaoh Amenhotep II. This is the story."

"When I was about your age, Tutankhaten, my father took me aside and told me this story. This was before my older brother passed into the other world. After I heard the story, I embraced it and the Aten, determined to devote my life to his service. Then my brother met with a fatal accident out on the desert."

"Here my father paused. I was never sure if it was sadness at the passing of his brother, or at the realization that his life did not turn out as he had envisioned."

"Amenhotep II and his Great Wife Tio lived in Memphis near the Giza Plateau. Their son Tuthmosis..."

"Your grandfather."

"Yes. Tuthmosis would often go out hunting along the Nile and near the pyramids and the great Sphinx on the Giza Plateau. They sought lions and jackals. Giza teemed with these and it was considered to be a great show of courage to kill either, as both were vicious animals. On rare occasions, ostriches were

also spotted. These big birds were highly prized for their beautiful feathers."

"Did he also fish in the Nile? I have seen the fish swimming there but we never eat them."

"Oh no, son. Back then, as now, the eating of fish was forbidden by the gods."

"Why?"

"Long ago when the gods and Egypt were young, Osiris fought with his brother Seth and lost. Seth then cut up Osiris' body and threw the parts into the Nile where the tilapia and abdju fish ate the evidence of his betrayal. Since then, all pharaohs and priests have been forbidden to eat fish out of respect for Osiris."

"When I become Pharaoh, I will not eat fish either, Father."

"That is good, son. One afternoon, rumors came to the palace that ostriches had been sighted near the pyramids. Early the next morning, Tuthmosis and his hunting party left for Giza, traveling by chariot. He hoped to come home with two prizes: a lion and an ostrich.

"After a long morning spent under the blazing sun and no sign of either animal or bird, the party took rest in the shadow of the great Sphinx. Tuthmosis chose to sit between the Sphinx's paws where its mighty head blocked more of Re's rays."

"Is that when the Sphinx talked to him?"

"Yes, it was. And this is what it said: 'Look upon me, my son Tuthmosis! It is I, your father, Horemakhet Kepri Re Atum. It is I who gives power over all Egypt. Both its White

Crown and its Red Crown shall sit upon your brow.'"

"The crown of both Egypts, Father?"

"Yes, my son."

'Then he continued the story."

"'You must clear this desert sand from my limbs and protect me from further damage. Long have I awaited your coming, my son. Forever will I watch over you.'"

"Then the Sphinx spoke no more."

"Ever?"

"Ever. But he had heard the god speak to him and knew these words to be true: He, Prince Tuthmosis, was the son of the god Re-Horemakhet. The god Aten.

"When he was made pharaoh upon his father's death, Prince Tuthmosis did as the great Sphinx asked. He cleared the sand and built a mud wall to keep out the desert during wind storms and down through the centuries. Then, he adopted the symbol of the Aten for his standard to honor the Aten."

"That's what we've done, Father. The sun with the rays coming out of it is on the entrance door of the palace."

"And many other places also, son. Prince Tuthmosis honored Horemakhet Kepri Re Atum, and he ruled for thirty-three years."

"I grew silent knowing that the Aten was truly powerful to allow Tuthmosis to rule that long."

"Since that time, the devoted worship of the god Re Atum has passed down from Tuthmosis to your grandfather Amenhotep III, to me, and one day to you. All of us are Sons of Re Atum, just like Prince Tuthmosis."

"After hearing that story, I imagined the Prince

sleeping between the Sphinx's giant paws and hearing the god talk to him. I could understand how important it was for my family to honor Re Atum. It wasn't until later that I found myself unable to continue that worship.

"Several days later, my father sent for me again. This was new for me, but had been happening more since the day my father acknowledged me as his son."

"Tutankhaten, I want to you understand when you are older, why I have acted as I have as the Pharaoh of Egypt."

"Yes, Royal Father."

"I became enamored with the story of Prince Tuthmosis and the great Sphinx. All I wanted to do from the time I heard the story was to serve out my life in the service of my god father Horemakhet Kepri Re Atum."

"Didn't you want to be the pharaoh?"

"No, it was my older brother's position, not mine. I was to be a priest of the Aten. But the gods had a different and harder path for me."

"What was that, Father?"

"I was crowned pharaoh upon the death of my father and the earlier death of my brother. I was expected to continue leading the people in the worship of our gods and maintain the Maat. But I could not."

"I remember looking at him, puzzled. Becoming the pharaoh of all Egypt seemed such a magnificent thing."

"Before Nefertiti and I moved here from Thebes, we were not happy. Ruling Egypt was something I was not good at, or

interested in. In fact, even now as we speak, Grandmother Tiye handles the majority of the duties. She has been doing so for quite a while now. Do you know why we left Thebes?"

"No, Royal Father."

"For the first time in my family's history, threats were being made against a pharaoh, and his family, rising from my perceived lack of leadership at the helm of Egypt. The situation was becoming too dangerous for us to remain in Thebes. There seemed to be no way to stem the tide of anger that was rising against us."

"Even at the age of six, I knew that this was very unusual and not even talked about outside of this room. In Egypt, the pharaoh is considered to be the embodiment of a living god. For Egyptians to voice, or even think, about harming their pharaoh was equivalent to voicing or thinking about harming their god."

"We also wanted to give our people a chance to know the power of the Aten, and we thought building a city to honor the god would help. It has not turned out that way. The people have become angry that Tiye is in charge of the armies and refuses to send them to protect Egypt's borders. But Queen Tiye is doing what I asked of her. Nefertiti has helped with some additional duties, but since we've moved here, she has been busy raising our children."

"I nodded as if I understood all that he told me, but some of it was beyond my six years."

"I love Egypt and her people, Royal Son, but I have never wanted to rule her. I hope that the people of Egypt and you

will understand that in time."

"I did eventually, but it was not until several years after this conversation and the occurrence of many other events." Tut falls silent, lost in the past.

Quiet surrounds us as I try to understand all that Tut has told me. I know some of the history, but not all this. I think of the boy so long ago who only wanted to follow in his family's footsteps and serve the Aten. Instead he answered the call to lead the strongest nation of his time. Because of that, he and his family were lied about and branded as traitors.

I look at Tut, leaning back against the stone, his eyes closed. What a burden to have placed upon his shoulders at so young an age.

"Did your people think that your father was a coward?"

He nods. "Many thought that. I believe that General Horemheb encouraged that thinking also."

"So," I say holding up my fingers. "One, General Horemheb did not approve of your father's military policy." I fold one finger down.

"Yes, that is true."

"Two, the people felt your father turned against all their gods." I fold another finger down.

Tut nods.

"Three, the people did not like this Aten god."

"It is true. My father was not popular with the Egyptian people because he chose to devote his life in worship of the Aten, god of the sun disk. But he did not turn his back on the rest of our gods. He just continued the worship inspired by Tuthmosis and the Sphinx. Many felt that this worship, combined with his refusal to arm Egypt's borders, disrupted Maat, the balance pharaohs were responsible to maintain."

"Because pharaohs were considered to be the gods. Right?"

"Yes."

"So why didn't the people do as he wished?"

"Some did, but as I see it now, they did so only to avoid his displeasure. I sometimes felt Father was as disappointed in the Egyptian people as they were in him. He expected them to respect and honor his commitment to the Aten. It is true that the temples in Thebes, particularly at Karnak, appeared to close down, but not through any orders of my father. When the people followed him to Akhet-Aten, few worshippers were left in Thebes."

"Did Ay and Ankhesenamun know this story?"

"Yes. Hesena heard this later from our father. Ay was Nefertiti's father, and he had to be aware of the story when he consented for Nefertiti to marry my father."

My brain is spinning now. I remember pictures I have seen of the Sphinx. It sits on the plains of Giza, along with the pyramids. Its nose was broken off at some point. Bet that was one heck of a fight.

I close my eyes to picture it clearer. I can sense Tut's wonder, but I concentrate hard. The picture forms in my mind. Huge lion body with a human head, fixed between two enormous paws. And there it is— what I am searching for.

"Did you ever go to the Sphinx?"

"No. Once Father was dead, Hesena and I ruled only for a short while in Akhet-Aten. At Ay's urging, we abandoned the temple of the Aten, moved the people back to Thebes, and took up the old worship. Ay had me appoint General Horemheb to govern Lower Egypt while he governed Upper Egypt." He pauses, his eyes sad again. "Our time in Thebes turned out to be too short to make the journey to the Sphinx. Why do you ask?"

"There is a sign in front on the Sphinx. Well, not a sign, but a stone..."

"Yes, a stela, we call it. Tuthmosis III had it carved and set there. My father and Nefertiti visited it before the move to Akhet-Aten."

"Did Ay know about the stela?"

"Yes, he visited there with my father." Tut stops. "That's it."

"What?"

"Before our move back to Thebes, Ay journeyed to Memphis and Giza. He mentioned visiting the Sphinx at my father's request. Maybe there is a clue there, at the Sphinx."

"At the least, it's worth checking out."

"Yes, we cannot stay in this time any longer."

"In this time?"

"I was allowed one trip back into my past, to bring you, to show you my life. Re consented, but now we must move forward to Horemheb's time. I will be unable to move us across the span of time again. We must find what we are looking for in the time of Horemheb's reign."

Clouds form in my head. How does one go from my time to Tut's childhood to Horemheb's time and move forward? I haven't a clue.

"How long will it take to travel to the Sphinx in Horemheb's time?" I ask innocently.

"About as long as for you to hold my hand," he says grinning.

"Great." I grasp his outstretched hand and hold on for dear life. OMG, this makes my stomach swim.

Chapter 9

My head is still spinning, and I'm
pretty sure my stomach is back at
Akhet-Aten. I'm as wobbly as a new-
born foal. Tut tightens his hold on
me as I get my walking legs back.

"Why doesn't this affect you?" I ask.

He gives me that cocked head and lopsided grin.
"I'm dead, remember?"

Great, he's picking up my sarcastic tone.

"Yeah, right," I reply. More steady now, I move
away to stand on my own. Tut walks away. "Hold up.
Where are we?"

"Look around, Roosa. Just where we should be."

In front of me is desert, sand, open sky, and heat
for as far as I can see. Already sweat is starting to run
down my face and neck. I thought gym class was bad.
I'm not even moving here, and it's as if a river is
coursing through me. I sweat more standing still in this
country than I ever did playing basketball.

Turning around, I stare at the sight in front of

me. The Pyramids. I've seen millions of pictures of them, but this is different. I'm standing here on the same ground, in the presence of these mathematical wonders. Perfectly shaped pyramids, over four thousand years old in my world. In this world, well over a thousand years old. And all around is desert. I twirl around. Nothing but desert in all directions. This can't be real.

"Tut, is that really the great pyramid of Khufu?" I ask, needing confirmation of where I am.

"I'm not sure it's great, but yes, that is Khufu's pyramid. And those of his son, Khafre, and his grandson, Menkaure."

Only momentarily does Khufu's monument dwarf the others. The sun's glare draws my attention to Khafre's burial pyramid revealing the one shining difference between our times. Here Khafre's tomb is covered in polished limestone; in today's world, only the crown remains covered. The rest has been stolen and re-used over the centuries. What I wouldn't give to touch those building blocks. To put my hands where ancient laborers laid theirs.

"Can we go closer? Can we climb up Khufu's?"

"Of course we cannot. That is forbidden. These are the resting homes of Pharaohs, Egypt's gods. We do not climb, but we may go closer," he adds. "Come, let us see the stela at the Sphinx, and then we'll go."

"Where is the Sphinx? I thought it was right here with the pyramids?"

"It is. Right there." He points to a huge mound of sand.

"No way. Where is it really?"

"This is it, Roosa. We are just around the back. Come, I will show you."

I follow him with difficulty. I don't know how he walks in all this sand without it getting into his sandals. My feet feel like they're standing on a million peas, you know like that story 'The Princess and the Pea'? I stop to dump the sand out.

"Come, Roosa. You must hurry. We haven't much time. Another day has passed."

"I'm coming. Just emptying the desert out of my shoes." I hustle to catch up with him and realize the peas are already back. "How do you walk in this without all the sand getting in your sandals?"

"I've had thousands of years to learn to walk the sands of my Egypt. You will learn."

"Not me," I mutter. "I'm not staying around for thousands of years. On the other hand, if we don't hurry, I might find the desert more welcoming than my parents."

"Here, Roosa. Here is the Sphinx." He points to the sandy hill. "Come, the stela is down here between its paws."

Something is wrong with this picture. This can't be the Sphinx. It's supposed to be gigantic. My head is nearly even with its chin. Where's the lion body? And the paws?

"Where are its paws?" I ask. Then I look up at its face. No way! "Hey, Tut. This sphinx still has its nose. This isn't The Sphinx."

"What are you saying, Roosa? Come and help me clear the sand away from the stela."

"I said, this isn't The Sphinx. It still has its nose."

"Of course, it has a nose. That's the way it was made."

"No. You don't understand," I protest. "The Sphinx in my time has no nose. It's been broken off for centuries."

Tut casts me a perplexed look. A tingling sensation goes through me like when you touch your tongue to the two terminals of a battery.

"Come, Roosa. We need to unbury the stela."

I follow blindly, still looking at the undamaged face of the Sphinx. It's definitely more striking to see it in one piece.

"People have always wondered what happened to it," I say more to myself than to Tut. "Guess I won't find out now."

It is only as I help Tut scoop the sand away from the top edge of the stela that I realize the sand has drifted and blown all around the Sphinx, burying it up to its neck in places. No wonder it appears smaller.

The desert always reclaims its own, even mighty Pharaohs.

I jerk my head up searching for the voice. I

glance at Tut, but he continues to dig.

My hands wrap themselves around my stomach. The nausea's coming back. It is her. It is Ankhesenamun.

"It is all right, Rosa. Here in my homeland I find communication easier for short moments."

Tut stops digging, his eyes glued on me.

"Please, Rosa. Show him I still love and support him."

Confused, I start to question her, but like an avalanche, the answer bursts into my mind. The picture at home in my room. The two of them. Her longing sits heavy in the pit of my stomach. Unable to do anything else, I nod ever so slightly. Then, with Tut's expression still questioning, I reach out and touch him as she does in the picture. Energy flows down my arm into my fingertips. Tut grips my hand and presses it to his heart.

"Hesena." His voice is but a whisper.

I nod, weak but strong at the same time. "She wants you to know that she loves you and supports you." I drop my gaze, embarrassed to be saying such words to a boy, even a dead one. Geez, I blush just trying to say hi to Caleb on whom I have a terrible crush.

Tut squeezes my hand once more. Hesena fades from my mind. Then he drops to his knees. "Dig Roosa. I fear we are close, and so is danger."

We dig furiously for several more minutes, increasing our efforts with each inch of the slate exposed. Finally, it lies bare in front of us.

There before me stands the story of Tut's great-grandfather written in ancient hieroglyphs. Hesitantly, I reach out to touch them. I trace the signs not knowing what they mean, but understanding the power they hold. The power to transform history with their message. "No one will ever believe this." I manage a short laugh. "I'm not sure I believe it."

Tut steps forward and blows on the stela. Sand flies everywhere, into my eyes, nose, and mouth.

Sneezing, I lift a hand to wipe off the gritty snot. I know, gross. Who would have thought to bring tissues here? Tears stream down my cheeks.

"Thanks," I say, still coughing and sneezing.

"Sorry."

"Yeah, right," I say, aware that his entire being is focused on reading the stela. Wait—reading the stela?

"You can read hieroglyphs?"

He gives me one of those looks. You know, the one the teacher gives when you ask her to explain that concept for the third time or to give the directions again.

"Right," I say. "It's your language."

He continues to read as sweat mixes with the sand on my face. Instant luffa. I don't recommend it. Instead of leaving my skin smooth, it irritates my sunburn.

Touching the top of my head, I wince. Sunburned, no, probably sunbaked before we're done here. Nice for a blond. My hair will be bleached white, and my head will be bright red. I need to cover my head before it blisters, and I get cancer. Wonder if the ancient Egyptians ever heard of melanoma?

Looking at my shorts and t-shirt, I don't have much to work with. Guess it will have to be my shirt. Using my teeth, I rip it at the bottom, and then tear it all the way across.

Left with a strip about five inches wide and a bit longer than my arm, I wrap it around my head unsuccessfully. It unravels, and I try again.

Tut stops reading and smiles at my antics.

"Here, let me." He takes the cloth out of my hands and wraps it around my head, tucking the ends under.

I shake my head. "Years of practice, right?" His lopsided grin is my answer, and then he moves back to the stela.

"Here it is, Roosa," he says, his voice vibrating with excitement.

I join him and look at the lone hieroglyphs down at the bottom, having been protected by the sand. "What does it say?"

"It says, 'This, Ay, Pharaoh of Egypt, write for those who follow. Horemheb continues to grow stronger. One day soon he will depose me and kill me. Against all the written laws of Egypt, he will take a pharaoh's life. He will deny me burial if he can and the rites due to me. Ankhesenamun has promised to save and hide my earthly body so that one day the respect due to me and Pharaohs Akhenaten and Tutankhamen can be given. Only she knows where my burial is to be. Only I, and one other, know where she will lie. I have entrusted instructions for her final burial with the most trusted person I know, Maya, Overseer of Works in the Place of Truth.'"

"Who is Maya?"

"A trusted friend of my family. He oversaw the royal tombs of my whole family. It is my hope that he outlived Ay."

"What about Ankhesenamun?"

He shakes his head. "I don't know. If Maya didn't outlive Ay, then Hesena may not be buried where Ay commanded."

Grimly, I speak what he would not. "If he didn't, then even Ay will not know where she is."

He says nothing but returns to his reading.

"'To the one who reads this, you are charged to find and honor me. You are charged to find Ankhesenamun and to assist her in restoring the honor of the Sons of the Sphinx: Thutmosis IV, Amenhotep III, Akhenaten, Tutankhamen, and Ay.'"

"He came back here after you died, didn't he?"

"Yes. Maybe only days before his own death."

Tut rises and walks a short distance away. His face clouds up, and he pounds a fist on his chest.

"How can I find either of them when only they

know where each is buried?" His voice cracks on the last words.

I start toward him, but suddenly I can barely take a breath. My fingers claw at my throat, and I try to call out, but only manage a croak. It is enough.

Chapter 10

Darkness clouds my vision, and dimly I'm aware of Tut running toward me. He slams into me, knocking me back into the sand. A deafening crash shakes my teeth and suddenly an avalanche of sand plunges down. I can't breathe; the grit is in my mouth and fills my nose when I try to inhale. Panic lends me the strength to battle the weight of the sand, not to mention Tut, who is still on top of me. Fighting for air only increases the pounding in my head. What in the world? My hands clutch at a solid object.

Strong arms pull me free, releasing a waterfall of grit that cascades over me lodging in the most uncomfortable places. Choking, I blink to clear my blurry vision. Tut brushes the desert out of my hair, off my face and clothes. Sand still clings to his skin and clothes.

"Roosa, are you all right?"

Not wanting to choke again, I shake my head then nod. Actually I'm not sure I'm okay. I have to go home before I die here.

I start to tell him this, but looking behind him, I just point.

Tut turns his head and whips his head back toward me, his eyes wide with disbelief.

The Sphinx has no nose!

I start to giggle uncontrollably and plop down in the sand. Tears stream down and suddenly sobs, not laughter, rack my body. I can't stop.

I don't know how long it takes to calm down. Tut just sits there beside me, his arm around my shoulders, whispering softly in a language that I don't understand, but deep inside, my soul recognizes the words.

Finally, I take several deep breaths and get myself under control. Tut says nothing, but removes his arm.

In my mind I replay what happened. I've felt that crushing grip on my throat before. "It was Horemheb, wasn't it?"

"Yes. I saw him at the top of the Sphinx. He brought his sword down on the top of the Sphinx's face. If you hadn't attempted to call to me, you would have been buried alive under *debens* of sand. I would not have been able to dig fast enough to save you."

I touch my throat, shuddering at how close I came to dying.

"He's not trying to kill you, only warn you away. With his magic, he could have killed you back at the palace."

"Well, that's nice to know." Sure felt like the end for me both times. I can't do this again. What if he changes his mind the next time? This is it. I am done, word or no word. Love or no love. Nothing here is worth dying for. I'm so far from home in more ways than one. I want to feel my mother's arms around me and have my father close by to protect me. The time of the pharaohs isn't all mystery and romance. In this harsh and unforgiving land, it's a time filled with treachery and danger.

"I want to go home, Tut, not muddle around in this ancient land where the boundaries between life and death fluctuate without reason. Where magic serves evil instead of making children laugh and stare in wonder. I don't know the rules here, and no one follows them anyway. My world isn't perfect, but it's better than this."

He starts to protest.

"Now. Dying in this Godawful sand and sun may have been okay for you, but not me." Sadness falls across his features. He closes his eyes, opens them, and looks at me.

"I will take you home." The dejection in his voice tugs at my heart.

"Why did General Horemheb try to kill—excuse me—warn me again?" I don't expect an answer, but one can always ask.

"He fears you. He fears her."

Instinctively I know who he means.

"She is the only one who can bring justice and death to his *ba*."

"Ankhesenamun," I whisper reverently. A warm tingle surrounds my heart. I know I stand no chance, not against her. I'm not brave, or any kind of a hero. I'm a fifteen-year-old girl who is afraid to talk to the boy I sit next to in the cafeteria. I must be mad. There is no other reason for the words that come out of my mouth.

"I can't go home, not yet." Relief flows over Tut's face like ice cream melting on a hot summer day. Note to self: When I am done here, no more thinking with my heart, only my head. And then I have to hope that I'm smarter than my grades show.

Peace settles over me and enlightenment shines from within. It was there all along. What we need to know, she has already told me. I reach out to him, resting my hand on his arm. In answer to his unspoken question, I reply. "It's me, Rosa, not Hesena. I know what she knows."

His eyes widen as he tries to figure out what I just said.

I try again. "Earlier, right after we got here. You remember?"

"Yes."

"She spoke to me. She said, 'The desert always reclaims its own, even mighty Pharaohs.'"

I hear him repeat her words over and over again.

"It is a clue, Roosa. Come. Let's go into the shelter of the pyramid while I think some more."

"Tut," I say, following him over the sand, shaking the desert out of my t-shirt wrap before putting in back on my head. Oh, one more thing: my feet are walking on those peas of sand again. "You won't let Horemheb harm me, will you?"

He looks back, still walking. "You are a special person, Roosa. I would sooner let him kill me. I will keep you safe."

"Thank you." It reassures me, although I know Horemheb will try again. After all, the general hasn't threatened Tut. Maybe because Tut is already dead.

"Tut, what were those words that you spoke while I was crying?"

I see his shoulders rise with a deep breath. He doesn't stop. I start to ask again when he speaks. The depth of his sadness overwhelms me.

"Twice in our life together, the hymn I sang to you, I sang to Hesena. Its words are old and full of magic. Twice, we lived through horrors that no one should ever experience. It was only those words that breathed life back into her soul, into our souls." He pauses and turns to glance briefly at me before continuing. "You needed those words to heal as badly as we needed them so long ago."

A lone tear falls from his eye. His face stiffens with pain.

Shoving my fist in my mouth to keep from

crying, I reach down inside me for the strength to continue. I have nothing to offer him in return for my life. Nothing but her.

I follow him in silence.

†††

We sit in the shadow of Kaufu's pyramid, leaning back against desert pillows that Tut made. He hasn't said another word since we sat down, lost in thought. Maybe about where to go next; maybe about the time he last sang that magical song to her.

Re is readying to move down into the Duat, the house of night. The Sphinx basks in the diminishing glow of the sun. Having seen it whole, I must say that it looks more imposing, more powerful without its nose. This monument to a pharaoh has actually seen the historic figures I've studied in school. Caesar, Anthony, Cleopatra, Alexander the Great, Napoleon—all household names today—passed by here. If there is magic in this world, it must start here.

Wish I knew what time it is at home. If I'm not home when my parents get there, they'll be worried. How do I explain to them what happened? Or an even better question is—should I try?

If Horemheb succeeds, and I die here, I wonder if I'll die in my own time also? Would I just disappear, leaving no clue as to what happened? My parents would never know the truth. I sit up straighter. That can't happen. I can't put them through that pain. Tut has promised to protect me. I only hope he can. This sounds like science fiction, except I'm the one in the story, not some kid who walks through a wardrobe, or who finds out he's a wizard, or even some kid from a galaxy far, far away. This is me, my life.

I brush away the tears on my cheeks. Leaning back against the sand, I gaze at the incredible scene that surrounds me—the pyramids, the unending desert, the Sphinx, and Tut. Shivers roll through my body, possibly from the desert chill as the sun sets or from the apparent hopelessness of our search, or both.

How *do* we find the tombs of two people when the dead are the only ones who know the secret? I close my eyes in weariness as a sigh escapes my sunburnt lips. I hear Tut breathing in the silence and then nothing as sleep takes me.

The pillow is hard. My neck feels like it has been knocked out of whack. Using my fist, I try to pound the pillow into softness. I strike once, twice, and then a vise-like grip seizes me. A voice penetrates the fog in my head.

"Roosa. Wake up."

A hand pushes my head, and I try to twist away.

"Stop. Leave me alone. I want to sleep longer."

"Roosa, you're dreaming. Wake up. We have to travel south. I know what Hesena meant."

"Crap." My eyes fly open. There beside me is my pillow: King Tut. "I'm sorry," I blurt out. "I must have fallen asleep."

"It's all right. But now we have to move. I know

where to go."

The floodgates open in my mind, and it all comes rushing back: Tut, the desert, Egypt, Ankhesenamun, Horemheb, Ay. "Where?" Eager to know, I'm also afraid that the General will tire of warnings if we continue on our quest.

"To the resting place of the pharaohs, where the desert reclaims her own."

Suddenly, I know also. "The Valley of the Kings."

"Yes, but in my time the Theban Hills were known as Ta-Sekhat-Aat, Great Field. Come, take my hand. We need to go to my Great-Grandfather Tuthmosis IV's tomb."

Oh, I hope my stomach can take this again.

Chapter 11

Either I've gotten used to traveling through this time wrap, or my insides have just given up complaining. Can't believe the last time I had water was in Akhet-Aten, sometime around 1335. Whoa! My head's still spinning, but at least with an empty stomach, I'm able to focus much sooner.

Tut has moved on ahead. The sun is just breaking over the Theban hills. His shadow lengthens beside him. Me? I just stand here and gawk. The Valley of the Kings lays spread out before me! The resting place of the mighty pharaohs of Egypt. This is desolate country—nothing but limestone, granite, sand, and sun. Although it doesn't look like much, there isn't another place like it on Earth, and I'm here. Not for the first time on this journey, I pinch myself to be sure I'm not dreaming. *Ouch!* No, not dreaming. Far above the valley floor sits the pyramid-shaped dome watching over these hills of kings. What would it have been like to have discovered an untouched pharaoh's tomb in here, like Carter?

"Roosa."

"Coming."

A well-traveled dirt road leads back into the valley formed by the hills on either side. Although not high by my experience, rising up from the sandy floor, the Theban Hills are impressive. Jagged crevices run up and down the sides of the hills, and in many places, man-made square arches can be seen. The Tombs of the Pharaohs. I'm walking in the footsteps of an ancient people. How cool.

I hurry to catch up with him. A mistake, sweat stings my eyes and grit scrapes my cheek when I wipe my face. My shirt is sticking to me by the time I come even with him. Does Re never find a cloud to hide behind? Did I say Re? Now I'm starting to think as an Egyptian. Good grief. Must be the heat. There is no shade anywhere. Like a shimmering mirage on a hot highway, the heat rises in waves off the barren hillsides. No trees can withstand this burning furnace. The only shelter exists under the entrances to the tombs.

Tut hurries ahead, but I may never get here again, so I take my time. We pass one entrance, and I walk over closer to it. Heavy wooden doors covered in hieroglyphs bar the way. Ancient rope—rough, scratchy, and strong—twisted around the door handles and knotted tight, holds them closed. On the right door handle there is a clump of mud molded like those wax seals used on letters. It covers the handle and the rope. Symbols are pressed into it.

"Tut, what is this for and what does it say?"

He hurries over, curious.

"Why the rope and this lump of mud?"

"Lump of mud? Oh Roosa, you are looking at the Necropolis Seal placed here by the priests. That it is still here means that the tomb is intact. No one has entered since the burial."

"Does the seal say whose tomb this is? Is it a pharaoh?"

"No, not a pharaoh. Here." He points to a set of hieroglyphs. "These state that this is the tomb of the dignitary Ramose." He pauses. "I remember hearing stories about him when I was young. He was the governor of Thebes during Thutmosis IV's time."

"Do all the tombs carry this seal?"

"Yes, but even in my reign, it was becoming difficult to keep the tombs sealed. Thieves continually broke in to steal the property of the dead."

"Tomb robbers."

"Yes. When they were caught, their hands were chopped off."

I gasp at such horrible consequences.

"You are shocked. I understand that in your time, there does not exist an undisturbed tomb here." He waves his hand around the entire valley. "Who are these people who think they have the right to touch a Pharaoh of Egypt, even a dead one? They disturb our sacred resting places and steal the items left for our journey into the afterlife. May they all be cursed along with their families."

I stand beside him, my mouth agape. Up to now, Tut has been determined in his mission, angry at Horemheb, but he hasn't lost his composure. Until now. I try to find words to soothe him.

"They only want the world to know about the pharaohs of ancient Egypt. How magnificent they were. How they lived."

He turns on me. "You don't learn about a people by stealing what is sacred to them. In my time and yours, they are nothing more than common tomb robbers!"

"Scholars have shared what they learned. They search for knowledge. I learned about you from the artifacts in the exhibit."

"Harrumph! What do you and they know? Nothing. Nothing at all! All you do is seek the treasures and the gold to make yourselves rich." He spits in the dirt. "You wouldn't know wealth if you were buried in it. Tomb robbers, the whole lot."

He stomps away almost at a run, propelled by his anger. I hurry to keep up with him. We round a bend and to the left a small path winds up a cliff and then disappears. His chest heaves with ragged breaths and he's actually vibrating he's so enraged.

"We aren't all like that, you know." I whisper, wanting to avoid a harsh response. "Some of us understand that true wealth comes from within, from one's heart, from love for others, and from respect for family." I pause. "Some of us do."

He says nothing; he doesn't turn to look at me, but his breathing slows; his fingers unclench.

He turns to me. "You are right, Roosa. The proof is standing here in front of me: you. Your life has been threatened twice and will probably be again, but still you stay."

"There are more like me, Tut, many more. There are others who seek only physical wealth, but people do grow up and learn. Most of those who broke into the tombs were acting like children left without adult supervision, who believed that the world revolved around them." When did I become so wise? "Sadly, they will never change. But others who came have been in awe and treated the dead pharaohs with respect and dignity. You above all should know that."

"He was still a thief."

"Probably so, but Howard Carter did treat you and your tomb with respect. He was so careful. And you are the only known pharaoh still at rest here, in this sacred valley." I finish my lecture which surprises me. Guess I've been getting more out of my project research than I thought.

Tut looks into my eyes. "You would have gotten on well with Ankhesenamun had you lived in our time. She, as you, was wise beyond her years." He pauses. "I'm not sorry for my outburst, just for directing it at you. I can hear her scolding me in my head." He chuckles. "Come, we have quite a task ahead of us."

I don't reply, but walk with him, knowing he is right twice. Today, we punish grave diggers in modern society. So why do we think it is okay to dig here? To disrespect the ancient pharaohs and their queens? Have we grown up at all over the centuries? Is history so important that desecrating the ancient dead is acceptable? In three or four hundred years, will people dig up my grave and justify its defilement for history? My brain feels full to bursting; one more idea to contend with and it may explode like an overripe tomato dropped on a hard surface.

Oh, the second time he was right? Ankhesenamun and I would have gotten along quite well. Quite well indeed.

Chapter 12

Tut leads us back in the hills of the Valley of the Kings to this cliff that looms straight up. If I have to climb that thing, I may just scream. I haven't done that in a while, have I?

I stop beside him. He is looking down, not up. At the base of the cliff is a depression and some faint outlines. No way.

"Are those steps?" Really? No way we have to dig down there.

Tut gives me one of those looks I've come to expect when I voice what to him is obvious.

"Yes," he says. He bends down and starts scooping out the sand which has buried the entrance to his great-grandfather's tomb.

Wish I could say that I didn't sign up for this, but I'm not really sure what I did sign up for. Joining him, we work side by side in silence, each of us lost in our own thoughts. At least that sounds good. I have no idea what he is thinking. Focusing on the task at hand and ignoring the sun beating on my back occupies my thoughts. I'll be lucky if I have any skin left by the time I get home. Notice that positive thinking?

Something keeps poking at my brain. Ignoring it, I concentrate on moving sand, now having to throw it up and over my shoulder as we go deeper. The stupid stuff sticks to my sweating hands and arms. Grit lands on me each time Tut throws sand over his shoulder; the hot breeze whips it over him and onto me. A couple of times I try to tell him, but all I get is a mouthful of desert. I cough; Tut pats me on the back like a baby and goes on digging.

"I thought the priests had a back passage we could use. You know, one that the people didn't know about? I thought I read that somewhere."

"They do."

"Well, don't you think that would be faster?" Breathing in the dry air brings on another coughing fit. Tut starts to pat me on the back. "Don't pat me on the back. I'm not a baby," I say, more annoyed than angry at all of this hopelessness.

Tut lowers his hand and looks at the steps. "Roosa, we have to get down to the seventh step. That is the doorway to the priests' entrance."

I stare first at him, then at the three steps we have unburied. "Four more? We've been digging forever, and we still need to go down four more steps just to find the door?" He nods. "Then I bet we have to unbury the door." He nods again.

I have no words. If you haven't noticed, this is a rarity for me.

Something else is wrong though. My focus wavers again like it did when we first started, the force inside stronger now. It's like watching a compass needle waver back and forth until it settles on North. Pain sears through my head. I think I just found North.

"Ow!" Wrapping my head in my hands, I swallow hard in an attempt to keep back the tears and stay upright. Tut cups my chin and looks deep into my eyes. Almost, it seems, into my soul.

"What, Roosa? What's happening?"

I try to speak, afraid it is Horemheb who has followed us here to this Valley of Death.

"No," I say to myself as much as to Tut. "Something is not right. I felt it when we first stood at the top of the steps, but I ignored it."

"What are you saying?"

I know now. The pain isn't from Horemheb; it's from her, Ankhesenamun. I dismissed her gentle hints, and she's sent the pain to get my attention. Dumb, huh? She could have just said, "Rosa, this is not where you need to be. Here, let me show you." Of course, she doesn't work that way. In some aspects, I sense her power in me weakening.

"She says this isn't it. We are at the wrong place."

"Hesena? You are sure of this?"

My hands go to my head again. "Oh yeah, I'm sure of it."

Tut slumps down on the step leaning against the limestone cliff. "I don't know where else to go. I don't know what she means."

The hopelessness in his voice stirs my heart.

"We have to think about it more. There has to be another place here, one more important."

He just shakes his head. Time is running out; I've been in his world for over two days. The next step has to be here in front of us. No, not those steps. We're—I'm, missing something.

Concentrating, I turn and look ahead where the Theban Hills rise before me, the resting place for dynasties of kings. We are in the right spot. That certainty sits like cement in my stomach. But, if here, and not here, where should we be? At whose tomb? Where would Ay have left another clue, certain that Tut's *ka* would find it, knowing that it would lead Tut to him and then to her? *Lead me*, I plead silently to Ankhesenamun.

A gentle force inside directs my gaze back down the trail. A picture forms in my head. A procession is making its way up from the valley entrance. Sounds filter through: weeping and the shuffling of feet carrying a heavy burden.

Looking down the valley, the picture in my mind plays out on the very path we took to get here. Twelve men struggle with the cart holding a gold sarcophagus, fit for a king. Following behind are nine people. At their head is a woman, more like a young girl, a teenager, dressed in night's clothing. The sable cloth flutters like raven's wings in the hot wind. She leans heavily on the arm of an older man who wears what I recognize as the double crown of Egypt.

Startled, I look closer. I've seen this before. Think, think. Where would I have seen this? No doubt this is a funeral, a king's burial, but whose? Slowly facts come to me. Only once in Egypt's history has a king taken the pharaoh's crown before the dead king was buried. Only once, but when? What did I read?

No way! I look over at Tut. He is watching me, a puzzled look on his face. *Is it possible?*

The reply comes softly, sadly. *"Yes."*

Sensing there is more, I ask out loud, "What are you not telling me?"

"His pain will be great, but if you help him, he can do it." Silence. *"He must do it, for us, for his family, for Egypt."*

The vision fades. Now the limestone hills stand before me.

I have another question. Tut stands beside me, saying nothing, waiting. He has heard my questions, but not the answers.

"Can we go there?"

"No. I will have to take you."

"You can do that?"

"It will require much strength, but if you hurry, I can. My power is waning. It weakens the closer the time comes to the

*day that I will be no more. The day Horemheb seals his line
with his son."*

"And I have to tell him?"

*"Tell him. When you do, take his hand, and I will know
you are ready."*

I'm trembling from head to foot unable to
believe this, any of this. I have to tell Tut that we need
to attend his funeral, his burial.

"What is it, Roosa? I heard you talking to her.
What did she say? Where must we go?"

How do I tell Tut he must watch himself be
buried and witness all the pain of his loved ones?
Every step on this quest gets harder.

"Hurry, Rosa."

I open my mouth. The words don't want to
come.

"Hurry, before I grow too weak."

"Tut, we have to go back...back to the day you
were buried here. We have to go back to your tomb.
Now." Before he can say a word and with disbelief
covering his face, I take his hand and whisper, "God
help us."

Chapter 13

Well, here we stand at the entrance to his tomb. How creepy is that? I've never even been to a funeral, let alone a tomb. I've been fortunate.

Tut hasn't moved or uttered a sound since we popped in here. He has this sick look about him. You know, when you've watched someone, or been that someone, who's stuffed his face with hotdogs, then goes and gets on the dragon ride at the amusement park. When you're almost straight up and down, it drops and your stomach rams its way up into your throat. Sometimes with predictable results. That's what Tut looks like.

I swear if he throws up, so will I.

"Roosa, you sure we have to go in?"

"Pretty sure that's what she meant. And I saw the, ah, your funeral procession, so I'm sure we go in." I reach for his arm; at least I think it's me. "I'll be right here. We won't stay any longer than necessary."

Tut nods. He takes my hand, and we walk

through the door not yet sealed and down the stairs. We see no one, and I'm hoping they have left. Although why the tomb is not sealed yet, I don't know.

The atmosphere inside is oppressive. Typical tomb, I guess. I wait for my eyes to adjust to the dim light. Already it's hard to breathe. The air is stagnant and smells stale, even dead, like the body it holds. The same one standing a few feet from me. Talk about weird. Can't imagine what it was like when Carter opened the tomb after nearly thirty-four-hundred years. The rotten air must have almost killed them.

At the bottom of the stairs, heavy wooden doors stand open. Ahead of us is a short corridor and then another set of open doors. Unlike Carter, who had to peek through a small hole to see inside, I find myself gasping at the whole room filled with real treasures.

The opulence is beyond any adjectives I've ever imagined. I close and open my eyes. Tut's treasures still sit in front of me. The golden animal beds I saw in the exhibit. Three of them, depicting the lion, the cow, and the hippopotamus with the crocodile's body. Over against one of the walls are the chariots, broken down and stacked neatly, ready for his use in the afterlife. Everywhere are chests of various sizes all carved with hieroglyphs and covered in gold and jewels.

I walk over to the cow bed. Made of wood and papyrus, it doesn't look very comfortable. Crouching down, I look closer at the items under the bed.

"No way," I murmur. "No way!" Tucked under

the bed is Tut's golden throne. You know, *the* throne. The one in the picture on my wall. The Golden Throne.

I run my hands over the golden lion heads on the front of the seat and down the legs that end in magnificent lion feet. On the arms are the jeweled serpent wings and the cartouche of Tutankhamun. I gasp as I lovingly caress the figures of Tut and Ankhesenamun sharing a private moment right here in front of me, not in a picture on my wall, but right here.

His wealth is abundantly evident: gold, jewels, rich cloths carefully folded, and the gilded statues standing guard. I wander around, looking, tempted to touch the rich gold, caress the sparkling jewels, but I don't. These are his treasures, his life. I must respect that.

Turning around, I open my mouth to ask a question but stop.

He is standing next to what looks like a small treasure chest. It is simple in design compared to the other items here. The container is painted blue; decorations in the form of scarabs, ankh signs, and hieroglyphs cover the lid. On the side is a set of four cartouches. I recognize Tut's with the sun disk of Re on top, the beetle Kherperu with the three lines underneath in the middle and the basket at the bottom. I saw that tons of times in the exhibit. I don't recognize the others. One must be Hesena's, but the other two? As I watch, Tut runs his hand over the lid and then lays his head down on the chest, his eyes closed.

Wait a minute. He's crying.

"Tut? Are you okay?" A tear falls from my eye. Brushing it away, I realize it is her, Ankhesenamun. These are her tears, not mine. Hesitantly I approach, knowing that what is in that chest affects them both. I touch his shoulder.

"Tut. Let's leave. There has to be another way to find Ay's tomb."

"Do you know what is contained in here?"

I start to answer, but realize he isn't really talking to me, more to himself.

"This chest contains the mummified remains of our children."

The breath whooshes out of me as if I've been hit by a semi-truck.

"You...you and she had children?" I look again at the chest.

The chest isn't that big. No more than eighteen inches. Their babies must have died at birth. I can't imagine anything worse. I like kids. One day, I'm sure that I'll have my own. But to have this happen. After waiting all that time, nine long months, to end up with a burial, not a celebration.

"What happened?" I whisper.

He never looks at me.

"Can you recall a time of great sadness in your life? A time when the burden on your heart threatened to break it in two? I had two such moments in my short life. Even today, thousands of years later, my heart still aches and my soul cries inside me when I remember those days.

"The first occurred when I was fifteen years and in the eighth year of my reign. Ankhesenamun and I had been married for three years, and we were expecting a child, an heir to the throne of Egypt!

"We were so excited at the prospect of being parents. How fortunate we thought we were. A child made from our love we could guide and watch grow. Someone we could love as we never were. We were also scared. After all, we were hardly more than children ourselves. But Ay and our vizier assured us of their total support. It is not hard to raise a child, we were told, when the whole palace helped with the raising.

"Alas, we did not have the opportunity to find out. Five months into her pregnancy, Ankhesenamun took ill. She lost our baby girl late in the night.

"The second time when I thought my heart would be torn apart was a little over two years later. Ankhesenamun and I were expecting another child. This time with only one month before the baby was due she began experiencing the birthing pains.

"After summoning help, I sat outside her chamber. Each little sound carried to my ears. I heard the doctor's commands to the midwives. I heard Ankhesenamun's voice distorted in pain. I heard Ay's heavy breathing at my side. I heard it all. Almost.

"I looked at Ay. His head hung down on his chest. His eyes could not meet mine. My breath refused to come. Tremors took over my body. I tried to stand, but my legs refused to obey me, the Pharaoh of Egypt! The ruler of the greatest country in the world could not even stand as the realization numbed my body.

"Later I lay down beside her and held her as sobs racked her wounded body. I cradled her in my arms, and my tears joined hers. I sang the song to her then, the same one I sang to you, to ease her broken heart, and mine."

I'm numb from the memory he has shared; all I can do is stand here stupidly. Tears flow down my cheeks and onto my shirt. I have no words to comfort him.

Tut comes over and brushes my tears away. Electricity jumps through my veins at his touch. My body. I think I may be getting in too deep here. I can't even tell if I was crying, or if it was Hesena, or both of us.

"Our lives might have been different if the children had lived. We would have been a family, and our children would have ruled Egypt after us. I might not have become so reckless. And we wouldn't be here now. Our name would be honored among the people, and Horemheb would only be a general."

The sigh that follows holds more regret than I've

ever heard one person utter.

"What changed?"

"Several months later I went ostrich hunting. Long after I should have given up, I continued. It was dusk when the dogs caught the scent. During the chase, my chariot hit a rock that Ahmose couldn't see. I was thrown; Ahmose was killed."

I put my hand to my mouth.

"I didn't know, but I was hurt, badly hurt, deep inside." He touched his chest to show me. "I was carried back to Thebes, unable to walk. Hesena had me laid in our bed. I never left it again, except to come here."

"Do you know that no one knows how you died?"

"You do, Roosa. But it matters little." He stops and squares his shoulders. "Our task is what is important now. Come, we must find Ay's clue." He dismisses me and walks between two life-sized statues into the next room. Once more he becomes that king, not the person.

I stand there a moment, gazing at the statues.

"Wonder who these are supposed to be?" I say out loud.

Tut's voice reaches me from the next room. "They represent my royal ka."

I move closer and touch one of them, running my finger along its smooth jawbone. "You know," I say, "these don't even look like you."

"Roosa."

I jump, not realizing that he has come to the entrance. He rolls his eyes and then those ebony orbs bore into mine. "You don't understand. Let's find what has been left and leave this tomb of sadness." He disappears back into the chamber.

"I want to understand," I say to myself. I go into the next chamber trying to remember what lay beyond. I would not have been more shocked even had I remembered.

Before us, nearly filling up the room and taller than either of us, stands the golden shrine of Tutankhamun. I remembered what else lay in that room. Inside that shrine are three more, each a bit smaller than the outside one. All tucked inside each other like those nesting dolls from my grandmother's childhood. Inside the last shrine were the four sarcophagi of Tut, each displaying him in golden and jeweled splendor.

The last one holds the famed mask of the golden boy. And beneath that, the body of the young pharaoh who now stands here before me. Beyond my understanding, he has been given back his human form, allowed to return one last time to restore honor to his family, one last time to find his true love. And here I am, trying to help, trying to understand, trying to stay alive. Will I ever be able to go home again? Or will I become as lost as Hesena?

Chapter 14

I put my hand on the outermost shrine. I really shouldn't, but it's hard to resist. The gold plating is warm against my palm, the sun's heat not having left its son's side. I am really here, inside this tomb open for the last time before being hidden for over three thousand years.

I glance around and back through the doorway. The shrine and the wealth are mind-boggling.

"Tut, you were rich beyond anything I can imagine. It's so unreal." I walk around behind the shrine. "You were one of the richest pharaohs in Egypt."

He looks at me and frowns. I see something in his eyes, briefly, that mirrors the disappointment in my dad's eyes the day the cops brought me home. I ditched school after one of those talking ghost episodes. They picked me up at the shopping mall an hour before school was out. An hour! I have all the luck. I cough as my throat tickles in an irritating way.

"Roosa." He sweeps his arm through the air.

"All this is here, with me, now, dead."

I suck in my breath.

"My wealth did not prevent my death. It did not bring honor to our family. It has not given me Ankhesenamun in the afterlife."

I lower my eyes, ashamed.

"Roosa," he says waiting.

I look up at him.

"This," he clasps his hands to his heart. "This is wealth, Roosa, the love Ankhesenamun and I have for each other. The sorrow we shared that is buried with me." He nods toward the chamber behind us containing the jeweled chest. "If I had remembered this on that fateful day, I would not have been reckless. I would have turned back to spend the evening with her instead of hunting. And Ahmose wouldn't have died."

"I'm sorry," I murmur. He is right. I reach out to touch his arm as myself, not as Ankhesenamun.

Understanding, he covers my hand with his, gently patting it. "Come. We must see what he is studying."

He moves and for the first time I see that we are not alone. At the end of the shrine stands Ay, the real flesh and blood Ay.

"Can he...?"

"No. It is as it was in my home. We are the intruders here. The gods veil us from his eyes."

"It's really...?"

"Yes, that is Ay."

He looks so much older than when we saw him at the palace in Akhen-Aten. Sadder and stooped over as if the weight of what he carries is crushing him into the ground.

Tut moves closer to Ay, and I follow.

Ay turns away from the wall and runs his hands along the shrine. He slumps forward, closes his eyes and lays his forehead on the top.

Tut moves next to the wall and gasps.

"Look, Roosa. See what is here!" He points to the painting of a group of figures clothed in white tunics and pulling a sled with the shrine of the dead on it.

"Is that your...?"

"Yes, my funeral procession. My burial procession."

His voice sounds odd. But then so would mine if I were staring at my funeral. I mean, how sci-fi is that?

Other figures clothed in long robes precede the sled pullers. Among them is a woman. In answer to my unspoken questions, Tut reaches out and gently touches the figure of Ankhesenamun.

"And over here?" I ask to draw him back. I point to another scene on the connecting wall that I don't understand.

"It is the Opening of the Mouth ceremony. Ay is performing *my* Opening of the Mouth!"

I look closer, studying the depiction of the boy, I

mean, the king standing next to me. I know how weird this has to be for him, but really? "Doesn't look that much like you," I observe.

Tut shoots me one of those parent looks that says, "Quit being an idiot." You know the one I mean. I shrug and wait for him to continue.

"It is rare to include either of these in a royal tomb. From the prophecy I know that I must perform the Opening of the Mouth for Ay as he has done for me." He pauses and crinkles up his eyes up. Thinking is my guess.

I wander back to the procession scene while he speaks. It fascinates me. I count eleven figures pulling Tut's sled. An odd number. Why not twelve like my vision?

Wait a minute. I drop to my knees. There is a twelfth figure! It is small and standing at the head of the sled. Why would he be there?

"Tut, why is this guy down here?"

He moves next to me. I watch his face. He stares at the procession, and then gets down on the floor next to me. He is so close, I feel the heat radiating off his body. Unconsciously, I lean closer before stopping myself. Whoa girl! My brain screams. I scoot over a bit. Tut doesn't seem to notice.

His fingers cover the twelfth person. Then he traces what appears to be a path through some curved lines. His body stiffens; he utters a sharp cry. He turns to me, excitement dancing in his crooked smile and shining through his dark eyes. His hands grasp my shoulders, their heat burning my skin.

"Roosa, this is it! This is the clue Ay has left. The one figure out of place. It is him!"

I force myself to concentrate, to draw my mind from the hands that still grip my shoulders. I force myself to repeat the words. "This is him? Who?"

"This is Ay, here!" He removes his hands to touch the figure again, but the heat doesn't leave my body. "And here, see the path he carved?"

I shake my head.

He grasps my fingers and traces the path carved in the limestone walls.

"Roosa, this is the map to Ay's tomb! Out by itself, by himself!"

I wait. This sounds like one of those word problems I can't ever seem to get in math.

Frustrated, Tut takes my hand and once again traces the line from the lone figure through the carved lines.

"Ay is not buried here in Ta-Sekhat-Aat, the Great Field. He is buried alone in the Western Valley beyond the far ridge!"

I shake my head.

"What Roosa?"

"All this," I wave my arm. "How in the world was all this supposed to come together?"

Tut tilts his head. "I don't know what you mean."

"Look at all this. A scheme or betrayal, or whatever it is, all concocted thirty-three hundred years ago to play out today!" I'm about to lose it. I attempt to walk toward the entrance, but end up only out of breath and have to stop. "How in the world did Ay know that you would come back? How would she know to find me? How could Ay know enough to write that message on the stela at the Sphinx and then to add these two drawings to your tomb?" My voice cracks as I try to keep from ranting hysterically. "What's going on? I don't understand any of this!" I sit down, silent, thinking of when Tut appeared in my room. Only minutes in my time, but we've been here for days. Impulsive as I am, it is only now that I ask what I should have asked then.

"Roosa, I can only answer you with what my father told me so long ago."

Our eyes meet, and I wait.

"Many forces inhabit this world. Not all are visible or good. Many shouldn't even exist." He pauses, taking in several breaths. "Look at you. You talk to dead people. How do you explain that?"

"I can't. And believe me, I've tried."

"Look at me. I've been dead for thirty-three hundred years, but I stand here today as human as you. How is any of this possible? I don't know either, but I've seen much in my first time on earth that I cannot explain. Sometimes, we just have to trust like my great-grandfather did when he heard the Sphinx, as you did when you heard me."

"But what or who are we trusting? Who is leading all of this?"

"In my time, I trusted in the Aten, Amun, and Re. Today you trust in one you call..."

"God."

"Or whatever name others of your time call the entity. Some things just have to be taken on trust and belief. That's all I can say."

I nod; he's right, but the uneasy feeling won't go away.

"Come, we must leave with Ay or be entombed in here until Carter comes."

"Why? You can just use your magic to time wrap us out, right?"

"No. We are in the Great Field of the Pharaohs. My abilities to time wrap are not present here. If I try to get us out of here, I could lose all power to protect you and take you home."

I shudder and follow quickly, unnerved that I didn't see Ay walk past. In the antechamber, we breathe a little easier, closer, even a bit, to the entrance.

Ay doesn't stop, but continues into the corridor. I start to follow, but Tut stops.

"Wait, Roosa. I need to find the crook to perform the ceremony."

I wait at the door, not wanting to search through his personal items. My ears track Ay's progress through the corridor and up the steps. Silently, I implore Tut to hurry.

"Here."

Tut holds a small shepherd's staff encased with gold and banded with what appears to be dark blue gems molded around the staff at regular intervals.

"Hold this. I need to close up the case."

I reach out to take the royal crook, judging it to be light. The weight of it brings me to my knees. I gasp, and Tut turns, a smile on his face.

"The tools of a ruler signify the heavy responsibilities that are embraced by all those chosen to rule. To be a pharaoh required total commitment from me and Ankhesenamun. The flail is equally as heavy. To hold both in one's hands showed the strength of the pharaoh. To waiver and fall as you just did, Roosa, condemned the people to a long hard life without any rewards."

"You were so young when you were crowned."

"Yes. Ay made me practice several hours a day in the last days of my father's rule. I had to be perceived as capable and having the strength to rule so the people would follow and believe in me. Remember, in my time, pharaohs were descended from the gods. And when the Sphinx spoke to Tuthmosis that day, we forever became the Sons of the Sphinx and the Aten who spoke through him."

We both turn at a sound—the door closing. I take off down the corridor, not bothering to worry about the lack of air. If that is what I think it is, we'll be dead soon anyway. I take the steps two at a time and never give a thought to whether Tut follows. Gasping, my head swimming, I leap up the last two steps and run into the closed and secured door to the outside world.

My fists beat upon the wood and between gasps, I cry out for Ay. "Ay. Wait! Come back!"

Chapter 15

Tut grabs my hands, now red and sore. "Roosa, it will be okay. Here, feel."

He guides my hands around the edges of the door. Without hesitation, I put my face against one side and breathe in the sweet hot air as it wisps through. For several minutes that's all I do: breathe. I hear Tut doing the same.

"Tut, we still have a problem. How are we going to get out of here?"

"Come morning, Ay will return with a final offering for my *ka* and *ba*. We can leave then. When he finishes tomorrow, Ay will seal the tomb for good. Come, let's sit and wait. It will be a long night."

We each take a seat on either side of the door. I sit for a while with my nose and mouth pressed against the crack in the door gulping down the air faster than it comes in.

Tut keeps his eyes on me. Probably wants to make sure I don't pass out. On the other hand, he could be looking right through me, not even seeing me.

I've done that.

Watching him out of the corner of my eye, I get a funny thought. This could be a reality show called 'Spend a Night in a Tomb with a Gorgeous Boy'. If so, I'd get voted off the first night because here I sit, nose pressed against the door jamb, my mind on breathing, not on Tut.

Time seems to stand still. It might be minutes or hours since the entrance swung shut. Tut has changed positions a couple of times. Me? I have barely moved. Yes, definitely voted off.

I catch myself giggling softly. The lack of oxygen must be affecting my brain. Nothing funny about dying of suffocation. The giggles continue. Clasping my hand over my mouth, I try to regain control. If my mother could see me now, she'd have a lot to say! The giggles are taking over and getting louder. Glancing at Tut's face, I see concern etched there. I wave him off with not one hand, but both.

My mother. Who would tell her that I was found dead in Tut's tomb? Carter? Would she even be alive to hear the news? The absurdity of my situation hits all at once. I break out in laughter, and then to my dismay, I am crying.

Tut comes over and puts his arm around me and draws me close. He murmurs words, but I don't know what he is saying. Maybe that same song from the Sphinx.

Slowly my brain unscrambles. I am in a tomb,

but Tut won't let me die here. Not only would that be the end of me, but also of his beloved. It would be nice to have him care that much for me, but I'm okay with the way it is, really I am.

I settle back in his embrace and close my eyes, content to know that for now, he is holding me.

✝✝✝

It turns out we don't have to wait for Ay. Sometime in the night, there are whispers outside the door. Putting his finger to his lips, Tut motions to me, and we make our way back down the stairs, through the corridor, and into the first chamber. The voices are faint, but the crack of the tomb door resounds down the corridor and echoes off the walls.

"What is that?"

"Tomb robbers."

"What?" I can't believe it.

"Usually guards are placed outside the doors of an unsealed tomb to prevent this, but Ay has not done that."

I step to the doorway for a better look. The voices come closer, and footfalls whisper on the granite steps. Then a pinpoint of light shows as if elevated in the air. They are descending the corridor.

"Roosa, go back into the burial chamber. I will take care of this."

"How?"

"Just go and keep quiet."

I bristle at his tone. There's that king voice again.

I do as I'm told, but I peek around the edge of the entrance and watch.

They come into the chamber, two men, one tall, one short. Their chests are bare; their tunics, once white, are now covered with dirt and soot. Ragged sandals barely cover their feet. I sniff the air and nearly gag. They reek of rotten garbage and feces!

"Look here," the taller one in the lead speaks. "I told you there would be lots of gold. This was a king."

The shorter man keeps glancing behind. "Let's hurry. If we get caught..."

"Shut up about that. I already told you we won't get caught. The guard wasn't set, and the old man won't be back until Re rises."

"That old man is now our Pharaoh."

I see Tut tensing at their disrespect.

"You think he's ever gone hungry? No. You think he's never had a bed to sleep in? No." The leader opens up his arms as if to scoop up the entire contents of the room and hug them tight to his chest. "This is ours. I spit on that boy who thought he would rule us."

He turns and spits in my direction. I jump away from the entrance.

"What was his is now ours! Give me a sack."

Tomb robbers, like these, are only interested in the monetary value of what they steal. I'm sure this scene played out in other royal tombs through the ages.

I peek around and see Tut moving close to the

leader. The anger in his face is plainly visible. Glad I'm not going to be on the receiving end of that.

The shorter one pulls two sacks out of a satchel at his feet. "Where do we start?"

"Look in the jars and chests. Pick the gold and gems easily carried."

The robbers show no regard or respect for Tut's things. They are completely consumed by greed, like a stray dog defending rotten food stolen from the trash. Unwilling to share and baring its teeth to anything that comes near. Jars stored neatly are dumped, the oils spilling out of them. Chests packed with clothes worn by the boy king in his youth are upended and the contents strewn around the room. Their hunger for treasure casts their caution aside.

When the leader opens another chest, his eyes widen as he beholds the treasure. Quickly he runs his hands through the necklaces and gems. As he turns to open his sack, Tut jumps over to the chest and slams the lid shut. Both men jerk as if shot.

"By the power of Seth!" Shorty shouts.

His face red, the leader scoffs and opens the chest again. "It slipped, you imbecile. I'll prop it open with some clothing."

No sooner does he say this than Tut once more slams the chest shut right on the man's arm. He howls like a wounded animal caught in a trap.

Shorty hurries over and helps lift the lid. "Look, I don't like this. Let's take what's on top and just get out of here."

Disgusted, the leader pulls his arm out and massages it. Red welts mark where the lid hit. "No! There's more gold and rich cloth in here than we will see in our lifetimes. We're not leaving it so it can rot along with the dead."

Not bothering to respond, Shorty drags his sack over and starts stuffing it with the cloth from the chest. As he puts the material in, Tut steps forward and pulls the same pieces out of the sack and throws them into the air. Already spooked, Shorty lets out a yell and runs for the door, his sandals beating a retreat up the corridor.

The leader starts to protest, but Tut picks up his sack and tosses it across the room. The man's eyes widen, and without waiting, he races after his partner. Their pounding footsteps echo back down the corridor.

Giggling, I step into the room. Tut eyes me, probably not sure if I've lost it again.

"Come, Roosa. They have opened our way out."

That king voice again. Don't think I like it when he uses that tone with me. Tut waits for me to leave. Not wanting to be told twice, I pass him and start my climb up the corridor again.

Behind me I can hear Tut chuckling, amused at the scene in the chamber. Those two men will probably never step foot in a tomb again, let alone entertain thoughts of robbing one. I'll even bet it will be a long time before they are able to close their eyes without reliving this night. I was scared we'd be discovered, and Tut was amused. I shake my head. Who would have guessed that the boy king would get a thrill out of a Halloween trick like this!

Halfway up the stairs I take my first real deep breath of fresh air. My lungs thank whoever, or whatever, is watching over us this night. Outside it is dark, and there is no sign of the two robbers. Probably halfway back to Thebes by now. The air is cooler here, almost chilly after the stuffiness of the tomb. I rub my arms to get rid of the goosebumps. My nerves are still a bit frayed also.

Tut has finally come and is inspecting the door. Fresh gouges in the wood mar the polished surface. Gently he closes it, and from nearby, he takes a stone and places it at the bottom edge. It's not a royal seal, but it works to keep the door closed.

"You realize that you have just given a reason for the curse that's said to surround those who come into your tomb, don't you?"

"A curse? Really." He chuckles again. "Maybe that's what kept my tomb hidden all these years."

"It probably didn't hurt." It certainly doesn't help to settle my nerves any. "Well, now what?"

"Well, Roosa," he pauses. "Now we have a problem."

"Really? Now we have a problem? Seems to me this has been one problem after another," I add. "So what is it this time? We know where Ay is buried. You still have the crook to perform the ceremony. I don't see a problem."

"It's the day of my burial, Roosa." He looks at me, expecting me to put the pieces together, but I only have one piece. Confusion must show on my face like it does when I try to make sense of those word problems in math. Mr. Stuart keeps telling me to put the pieces together to solve it. Even given all the pieces in math, I still can't figure it out.

"Roosa."

I say nothing because I have no clue.

"Roosa," he repeats. "We can't go to Ay's tomb and perform the Opening of the Mouth because Ay isn't dead. I am."

"Oh." That is a problem. "You're sure you can't do that time wrap thingy?"

"No. And even if I could time wrap inside the Great Field, it wouldn't help."

"What do you mean?"

"I mean, I was given special access to visit the year of my father's recognition. To show you. And, after that, I am only permitted to visit the year thirteen–oh-one with you. It is as the gods wish."

"Wait a minute. We're here now, at your burial." Oops. "Sorry."

Tut nods.

"It's thirteen-twenty-four."

"Yes, but look where we are and how we got

here." He pauses. "It was thirteen-oh-one when we entered the Great Field." He looks at me waiting for me to understand.

Sorry, I can't help. I'm lost.

"We are here now because Hesena brought us here. Have you felt her since?"

I shake my head.

"Inside the Great Field, the dead have little power. I don't know how she got us here."

"What if we leave, walk outside of the valley?"

"It will still be the day of my burial. I cannot take us to a different time. We only have three days left."

"What if we go back to my time, to my room? Couldn't we do that and come back after Ay has been buried?" Sounds logical to me.

Tut shakes his head. "Once we go back to your time, I cannot come back with you. And you must be with me when I find Hesena's tomb or we cannot be united in the afterlife. You carry her *ba* inside you. It must be there to let her *ka* join mine."

"Great. We're screwed."

I sound pretty calm, don't I? But I'm not. If bringing us here weakened Hesena's power, then she will not be able to take us back to 1301. I drop down in the dirt. If she can't take us back... I'll never go home, never see my mom and dad again; never grow up. Tears fill up my eyes. Blinking hard, I'm determined not to cry. It won't help, but I'm not sure what will. It sucks to come this far, only to fail. High above us, the black sky is lit by a million stars. Up there is Tut's god, maybe even my god. Up there has to be help.

Scooting back against the tomb door, I focus on the sky, our only salvation. Tut sits down next to me. The disappointment and frustration is plain in his frown and wrinkled brow.

Not for the first time, I wonder, why me? Why did Hesena choose me? How did Tut know to come to my room? Nana said sometimes there were no answers, but still I wonder. Maybe whoever or whatever guided Hesena and Tut to me will help us out of here. My eyes are heavy; my head falls; exhaustion takes over.

Chapter 16

Tut says that the new day is about to start. He can figure that out somehow by looking at the sky. I can't even tell the time of day when the sun is out, let alone at night.

My head itches, and I scratch it. My scalp is burnt so bad it's already starting to peel and itches like crazy. I scratch again, but this time a jolt of electricity runs up my arm.

"Whoa!"

"What is it?"

"I just got a shock. Static electricity, you know, from the dryness." I grab my head as the same shock wave reaches my brain.

Rosa.

The voice is weak, but it is her.

"Ankhesenamun."

Tut clamps his hand on my arm.

"It is her?"

"Yes."

"What does she say?"

I shake my head. "Nothing. It's almost like she is trying, but it is a struggle."

"Roosa," I hold up my hand, and Tut stops.

"I can take you back to when I found you. I would not leave you here stranded. However, it is the last time. I will not be able to contact you again. This will take all my power. Quick, grasp his hand."

I grab Tut's hand. He starts to talk, but the violent shaking of my head stops him. I squeeze his hand to convey what is happening. He tightens his fingers and brings it to his lips for a quick kiss. His eyes lock with mine, and I'm drowning. My heart is racing and then...

✝✝✝

I'm lying face down in the sand.

"What...in...the...world?" I spit out sand with each word. Pushing myself up with my hands, I sit up and brush off the grit. Tut is doing the same.

"What happened?"

Tut shrugs his shoulders and stands up.

I do the same, and let out a yell. "Look!" I point behind Tut, and he turns. The tomb entrance is gone. If I didn't know it was there right in front of us, there would be no way to know now.

Tut walks over and tries to clear away some of the sand to no avail. There appears to be large pieces of broken granite buried in the sand. He looks upward, and I follow his gaze.

"So, that's how you did it, Ay," Tut said, laughing softly.

"How he did what?"

"Hid my tomb. He started a slide up there somewhere. You can still see the faint path the sand and rocks took." He laughs again.

"I get it. He buried all traces of your tomb under the slide," I say with amazement. "Wonder if he had any idea that you, ah it, would not be found again for eons?"

"You can ask him soon."

I nod, but then what he said makes its way to my brain. "Are we there? The same time as earlier?"

"No way to tell for sure until we find Ay and confront Horemheb, but Ankhesenamun wouldn't get it wrong," he adds. "Come. Let's find the path to the Western Valley."

I take one last look at where his tomb was. Amazing. I'm the only one who really knows how it stayed undiscovered for so long. Amazing!

"Roosa, come."

Great, there's that king voice again.

†††

Well, here we are again. Tut, several yards ahead of me, moves with ease over the sand along a faint path. Me, once more I find myself plowing through the sand, stopping frequently to empty the desert from my shoes. If that's not enough, water's pouring down my entire body. The bottom of my t-shirt tied over the top of my head is soaked and only keeps the sun from searing my brain. If nothing else, I have to get home in time to shower before my parents get there. Unless, of course, the time wrap cleans me up. Now that would be something.

We have been climbing steadily for a while now. Somewhere ahead of us lies the Western Valley in this field of tombs and Ay's resting place. Hopefully, the answers we need are there too. Time is running out for us and for her. Since bringing us to this time, I have felt nothing inside. I shudder to think what will happen if she is gone; I mean really gone. Will Tut disappear also? Will he forget to take me home? I laugh softly. Not likely. After all, how can he forget about me after all the complaining I've done? Between you and me, that's the only way I can deal with the frustrations I know we both feel and with my fears. Fear of not going home, fear of General Horemheb, fear for Tut, and fear for her.

I wonder at times if my feelings for Tut have weakened her. I don't know if he's aware of them, but she must know. Hesena can't approve, but she hasn't punished me. I mean, it's not like I wanted this to happen. We have been together for almost four straight days here.

It wouldn't work between us. I know that. I'm not an idiot. He loves Hesena, and she him. I can feel that.

Sighing, I shake my head. I can just hear the

conversation with my mother if I told her of my feelings for Tut.

"Rosa. You can't love this boy. You're too young to know what love is. And he just wouldn't be right for you. I mean, he's so much older."

Older! Only by about three thousand years!

"It's your first experience with boys. It's called a crush. You'll see. You'll outgrow it and will thank me later."

Well, this may be a crush, but just try to tell my insides that when he looks at me with those dark eyes and touches me. Why does growing up have to be so complicated?

"Roosa."

I come out of my daydreams to see Tut stopped ahead. I hurry up to him.

"There," he points.

The path leads down to a small valley. At the far edge is a tall cliff wall. From this distance, it is easy to see a disturbance in the natural contours of the valley. Rocks and sand are strewn around in unnatural patterns.

"That's it?"

"Yes. That is where Ay waits." He takes off at a fast pace.

Following, I silently wonder if someone else also waits. It's been a long time since we've heard from Horemheb. Maybe his magic, like Tut's powers, can't work in this valley. Or, maybe he's just been waiting to get us all together. Either way, I can feel those footsteps my grandmother talked about approaching my grave again.

Chapter 17

We both stand there staring. Tut's disbelief must match that on my face. Before us, the entrance to Ay's tomb stands. In a shambles.

The heavy wooden door held together by a thin rope. One door barely attached to the frame. Broken shards of glass and pottery litter the ground in front.

"Who would allow this?" I ask already knowing the answer. "Ay was a pharaoh."

"Horemheb." The one word reply, full of disgust, is punctuated by him spitting on the ground. Quite gross to me, but evidently not to a pharaoh. Not sure at this point if I could even manage to spit, my mouth is so dry.

"Come." He unties the flimsy rope, lets the doors lay back against the sides of the hill, and leads the way down steep rugged stairs. After traipsing through a long corridor and down another set of stairs, we come to the entrance to a small chamber. Silently we approach. Somewhat hesitant, Tut stops and peers inside.

"Anything?"

"No. Just more fragments of pottery and glass on the ground."

I follow him through and utter a surprised "Oh." The walls are bare. No beautifully decorated walls or hieroglyphs of any kind. How strange.

Tut stands at the next doorway. The anger inside him matches whatever Egyptian curse words come from him.

On the opposite wall, which should have been intricately decorated, stand several defaced figures. Some have their faces dug off, and others, their bodies or limbs. The figure in the middle only has a mouth, stomach, and legs remaining.

"Is that Ay?" I ask pointing to it.

"Yes, with his *ka* behind. Those others are Osiris, Hathor, and Nut, the sky goddess."

He strides across to another entrance on the side and when he returns, the clouded expression covering his face tells me what he has found.

"Gone! Everything is gone!"

I hear him, but my attention is riveted on the large stone box in the middle of the chamber. Carved and etched into the red stone are funerary decorations in pictures and hieroglyphs. Each corner of the sarcophagus is embraced by a different god, their arms outstretched toward each other as if to shield and protect the body within. A half rounded granite top totally covered in hieroglyphs sits on top. Heavy gouges and scratches along the bottom of the lid show the determination of others to open Ay's last resting place.

"Is his...his body still in there?"

Tut walks around the sarcophagus, closely inspecting it. "The seal on the sarcophagus is not broken," he declares. "He is in there, for now."

"And now?"

"Now I perform the ceremony denied him upon his death which will allow his immortal body to continue living. To send his *ba* to join us in righting what has been done wrong," he pauses. "To allow his *ba* to reunite with his *ka* for ever lasting peace and health... what?"

Tut must have noticed my strange expression at his words. "He's going to join us? What does that mean?" I shudder to even venture a guess.

"If Ay's *ba* is to be one with his *ka*, we first have to confront Horemheb and see justice done," he says in that king voice of his.

"But, I thought there would be a clue here to tell us how to find Hesena. Not another ghost." I didn't expect this.

"The clue to find Hesena rests with Ay only. It is not drawn here, and even if it were possible that he left a written record, we would not find it." He motions to the defaced walls.

"Oh."

"Be not frightened, Roosa. Regardless of the tales told about Ay, he will not hurt us. When he returns, his anger will be directed at the one who allowed all this to happen." He gestures once again around the tomb. "His coming will fulfill another piece of the prophecy."

"Okay," I say somewhat hesitant. I have other questions that I have to ask; sure I won't care for the answers. "Will...will I be able to see him?"

"Roosa, Roosa," he shakes his head. "Of course you will," he says as if it is a natural occurrence.

I swallow and continue, "Will...will he be able to see me? To talk to me?"

"Yes. Just as you and I see each other and talk to each other, though Ay is more formal than me. If he desires, he will talk with you, but do not be disappointed if he does not."

Yeah, like that will happen.

"He was old when he took the throne and set in his ways, much like my father."

"What will he look like? I mean, you...you look like you must have looked when you were...alive," I stammer.

"I understand what you are trying to say. The Aten, Amun, and Re will allow him to return as he looked when he ruled, just as I am allowed."

I nod and take several deep breaths to calm my nerves. Okay, Rosa, I say to myself. I can do this. I have to do this. Can't be any worse than getting turned down by Caleb when I asked him to the dance. I didn't fade away or die. I won't here. At least I hope not.

"Stand by the entry way, Roosa, while I perform the ceremony. Prepare yourself for the sudden appearance of Ay."

Really? Prepare myself? How does one prepare for the appearance of a ghost?

Tut turns to face what is left of the picture of Ay and the three gods. As an afterthought, he looks over his shoulder and flashes that rare lopsided smile of his that burns like an arrow piercing my heart. "And Roosa, try not to scream. You might scare him." He winks at me before turning away.

Try not to scream because it would scare Ay? What in the world is he thinking? How about Ay not scaring me? He's getting pretty good with the sarcasm. I huddle in the doorway, ready to take off back up the stairs if Ay even looks at me wrong.

Tut removes the jeweled crook from his bag. His eyes close, and his lips move. I can't hear him, but it might be a prayer of some sort. Maybe to make sure nothing goes wrong. He raises the crook and touches the wall where Ay's mouth would have been had it not been dug out. He speaks in the ancient Egyptian tongue, but somehow I can understand every word.

> *"Hail Re, Lord of all.*
> *My mouth has been given to me*
> *so I may eat and speak with it*

in this world and the next."

Tut moves the crook up to where Ay's eyes should be.

"Hail Re, Lord of all.
My eyes have been given to me
so I may see on the journey you have given unto me
in this world and the next."

Tut touches the crook to Ay's ear.

"Hail Re, Lord of all.
My ears have been given to me
so I may hear the truth
in this world and the next."

Next, Tut touches each of Ay's arms.

"Hail Re, Lord of all.
My arms have been given to me
so I may find my balance
in this world and the next."

Last, Tut's crook touches each of Ay's legs.

"Hail Re, Lord of all.
My legs have been given to me
so I may walk the path of truth

in this world and beyond."

Then Tut kneels.

"All this, Lord Re,
you have granted unto your faithful Ay.
As the truth is seen,
Rise up and with your magic,
Protect and guide Ay from the evil magic of others
in this world and beyond."

Tut bows his head.

There is no puff of smoke, no lightning bolts, no fanfare. One moment Tut kneels before empty air; the next he rises to greet the *ba* of Ay.

I don't scream, but I jump and grab onto the doorway for support. A regal old man has materialized. His skin is wrinkled and browned, and he stands several inches above Tut. Like Tut, Ay is thin. No extra pounds on either of them. Around his waist a bronze tunic reaches down to his knees. Covering his chest is a matching bronze vest. Both are embroidered with jewels and gold. A highly decorated half collar encircles Ay's neck. Even in the dim light of the tomb, the blue, red, and green stones shimmer as does the gold.

Ay stares for a moment at Tut, then lifts him and embraces him. I swear I see tears glistening in Ay's eyes. The two converse for several moments in what I take to be ancient Egyptian, but I don't understand any of it. However, even if they spoke in modern Egyptian, I wouldn't have understood. I've been told I don't have an ear for languages, which must be true. Even in high school Spanish I can't remember how to pronounce a word after a few moments. There must have been something special about the Opening of the Mouth ceremony that allowed me to understand the words.

Several times anger creeps across Ay's face at Tut's words. Once he grips Tut's shoulders so hard that I expect to see bruises. Then both of them turn in my direction. Tut motions me forward. Unsure of my reception from Ay, I inch my way over to them.

Maybe because Tut is closer to my age, I frequently forget that he is a pharaoh of Egypt, except when he uses that tone with me. Now, Ay. That's altogether different. The power he once held envelopes me as I draw closer on shaky legs. Then, as if with a will of its own, I find my body kneeling before him, my head bowed.

Strong hands on my arms raise me, but I keep my head down. A chuckle comes from Ay and words I can't understand. He lifts my face until my eyes meet his. In those blue orbs, I find compassion and kindness, not the dismissal I had envisioned. He repeats his words again. I look to Tut.

"Roosa, Ay says that a daughter of his need not kneel before him. I explained all you have done for us as well as the problems we have encountered. His reply was that even if you did not carry the *ba* of his granddaughter, he is grateful for what you have endured and for your assistance. He has proclaimed you forever a friend of the Sons of the Sphinx."

I smile at Ay to show him I understand, and then tilt my head toward the entryway. Coming down the corridor is a roar that picks up speed and volume as it nears. That feeling I had earlier of being watched explodes inside my head. Panicked, I turn and run, forgetting about Tut and Ay.

Chapter 18

Outside the chamber, I cover my ears. The noise is deafening. My ears are ringing with the screech and crash of falling stones. It has to be Horemheb causing this, but I don't care. I *will not* be trapped in a tomb again. Ever! And that's what he is trying to do. Rocks and sand rumble above my head; the realization he's triggered a cave-in to trap us makes my head spin. He plans to kill us this time!

A shout from behind makes me turn. Tut is running after me, but it is not his voice that ignites the terror in my heart. It is mine screaming to hold on to life.

"No. No. NO!"

The force of the explosion flings me through the air like a rag doll. By the time I pick my head up a dense cloud of dust engulfs me. Too late I cover my face.

I'm choking, can't breathe, can't see! I'm dying!

Arms encircle my chest pulling me backwards.

My legs scrape painfully across the debris-covered granite floor. Another pair of arms lifts my legs. Floating. That's what it's like. Dying is like floating on air.

My body touches solid ground. Voices, whispers really, penetrate my clogged brain. I hope this is heaven.

Without warning, I start coughing and gagging. My brain screams at me. "Fight! Breathe!"

Arms shift me into a sitting position. Pounding reverberates throughout my body. My heart must be ready to explode. Still coughing and wheezing, my eyes open. Ay stands in front of me, terror on his face. The pounding doesn't quit. Where's Tut?

"Come on, Roosa." I hear him say. "Breathe, breathe."

The pounding increases. It is not my heart, but Tut trying to pound the life back into me. Reaching behind me, I grab his hands. "Enough," I choke out between coughs. "Enough."

No more pounding. Tut's face appears in front of mine. A little out of focus, but concern is etched deeply on his dirt-coated face. Tears stream down my cheeks; my eyes burn from the dust. Gently he wipes the tears away and then roughly pulls me to his chest, threatening to suffocate me and finish what the cave-in started.

"Roosa," his deep voice cracks, and he tightens his hold. "Roosa, I thought you were gone." This last utterance carries with it a sob.

For a moment, I drink in the tenderness, the caring, and the comfort I find in his embrace. Cherishing what I could easily interpret as love. Feeling what he and Hesena share with each other. Her silence means I am losing her—he is losing her.

I push myself out of his arms, reeling as I stand. Still gagging, I grab the rag from my head and wipe my face. This is the straw that breaks the camel's back, as Nana used to say. "I...have...had...it!" I spit out each word and punctuate the last word with the stomping of my foot.

"I know, Roosa. I'm sorry."

"No! This is it. This is the last time! He will not win!" Tut and Ay both look at each other, probably wondering if I've lost my mind. But I haven't, not this time.

A fit of coughing stops my screaming. Tut starts to pound on my back again. I push his arm away. A hurt look crosses his face. Ay still stares, unable to comprehend my ranting. "You ask Ay if there is another way out of here. A back door."

Taking one look at my determined expression, he turns to Ay. I hear the questions and from the nodding of Ay's head understand the answer.

"Okay," I say before Tut can tell me. "It's time for revenge, time to find Hesena and put an end to Horemheb's betrayal." Tut continues to stare at me, but I see a hint of that crooked smile of his through the dust on his face. "Tell Ay to lead the way."

Tut turns to tell him, but apparently Ay can read my body language as he is already heading down the corridor. He leads us through the burial chamber and continues on through to a chamber beyond. I grab Tut's arm as we follow.

"He did tell you where she is, didn't he?"

I've never really seen a person's face light up. Thought it was just an expression until now. Tut's ebony eyes glow. His grin becomes a laugh.

"He did, Roosa. He did!"

"Then let's go and get her, and bury Horemheb!"

✞✞✞

Re is rising over the east bank of the Nile. The walk out of the Valley of the Kings took the last hours of night. Ay's back door left us quite far back of the original opening.

Tut and Ay stand talking with their heads together. I take a moment to sit and catch my breath. I'm not that out of shape, but this heat is killing me.

Two days are left before Horemheb succeeds. But he won't. I know, I've moaned and groaned my way through this whole ordeal. No more. I've had enough. With that last attempt to kill me—kill us— something snapped inside. I may hear dead people, but I'm not ready to become one!

I'm determined to see Tut and Hesena together again as they should be. My heart tightens in my chest.

It's not for me that he longs. It hurts, but it can't be any different. I know that, but it doesn't take the pain away.

Pushing those feelings aside, I struggle to my feet. Once we find her, Horemheb must be set straight and honor restored to the Sons of the Sphinx. And then it's time for me to go home.

Tut and Ay have finished their conference. He and Ay embrace. Ay nods in my direction and then walks away.

I open my mouth to ask where he's going but Tut stops me.

"Ay has to leave," he says. "He will meet us at her tomb."

"Where?"

"Where no one would think to look, not even me," he says, raising his eyes to the sky.

I wait, hardly breathing.

"Where her father could protect her."

Confused, I have no idea what he is saying.

"Ay put her in Akhenaten's tomb behind a fake wall to hide her from Horemheb."

At first I think, *Oh no. Not another tomb to find,* but the excitement in Tut's voice says different. "Okay. Where do we go?"

"Back to Akhen-Aten. Akhenaten is buried in the hills west of the city."

"What are we waiting for then? Time wrap here we come, right?" I hold out my hand.

Chapter 19

We are lying in the middle of rubble. My stomach hasn't arrived yet. I may be ready for revenge, but my insides only want to be done with these time wraps. Ugh. Holding my belly, I lurch to a sitting position. Tut, already standing, looks around. He bows his head. I see his lips moving.

Still weak, I struggle to my feet weaving as I find my balance. Once my stomach arrives, I see what Tut sees.

Almost nothing is left of this beautiful city as I first saw it. What happened? Where the white-washed houses and buildings stood, little is left except a single row, not continuous, of bricks now brown and pitted. I can't believe this. I turn around looking for the palace. In the distance I see what remains: tall pillars marking the entry gate. Beyond those, the high walls ornately decorated with scenes of the royal family show signs of neglect. Several are missing bricks at the top, and the colorful pictures are marred by the attempts of others to destroy them.

Where we are standing tiles that were once part of the road stick out of the dirt. Of the low wall that separated the road from the walking path, nothing remains. And the walls displaying the identity of the houses, especially the one Tut translated, are obliterated as well.

The once magnificent city has been reduced to a ghost town. Not even that really. Ghost towns at least contain structures that the ghosts and human visitors could actually roam through. Not a whole structure is seen anywhere.

"Tut?"

"Ay told me I would be shocked, but I didn't expect this...this nothing."

"Did Horemheb do this?" I ask, dismayed that one person could so completely wipe out an entire city.

Tut shakes his head. "No. This is not the general's work. No. This is the work of my father. Of Akhenaten."

"What? How could he do this to a place he built and loved?"

"You misunderstand. He didn't do this. It was his haste in having his city completed for his family that caused this."

"Huh?" I'm struggling here with those word problems again.

"All those monuments of my Egypt that are still in your time, those that survived? The people built those of granite and limestone. Akhenaten didn't want to wait for barges to ferry the granite and limestone from the quarries. He had the people make bricks of mud from the banks of the Nile. Once baked dry by the sun, the bricks were used to make the buildings, houses, shops, and the palace. Then those were white-washed to protect them."

Now I understand. I built huts and mud pies when I was a kid. Left alone, those started to disintegrate in a couple of days. Cared for each day by adding moisture and more mud, they would last all summer. The people of Akhen-Aten achieved the same result by white-washing the bricks frequently.

"Once Hesena and I left for Thebes, the people followed. No one was left to care for my father's city. And just as we once more embraced the Amun above the Aten, so the city of Akhen-Aten fell into ruin."

"But did you have any idea..."

"No. We needed to restore Maat in the country, in the people, in ourselves. We did not return."

"Wow." I can't think of anything else to say. There are no words to describe what lies before us.

"Come. We need to go to the Royal Necropolis and find Akhenaten's tomb. I cannot fix this." He waves his arm at the remnants of the once powerful city. "I can restore Father's honor. Come, Roosa. Time grows short."

His tone indicates the discussion is over. That king voice again. I follow him through the ruined streets, but my thoughts still carry on the discussion.

Only now do I understand what a task he has set for us. How do we restore honor to the man represented by all this…this destruction and decay? This reaches further than just Horemheb's betrayal. This goes back to the beginning of the Aten as god, back to Tuthmosis. It has now become a struggle between one ruler and his god and the people and their gods. This is a battle of a man determined to honor his heritage and fulfill the commitments forced upon him with the death of his brother.

✝✝✝

We stop at the base of the cliffs which encircle the city on three sides with the Nile behind us. Tut is surveying the surrounding area.

"There." He points to our left. "There is the path Ay told me about. It leads up to the Royal Necropolis. Come."

"Wait. Akhenaten's tomb is up there?" He nods. "But Egyptians buried their dead west of the Nile where Re dies each night. Everyone knows that."

Tut sighs and his shoulders sag. "My father did not follow tradition as you know. He was a confederate of your time, you could say."

"What?" Oh no, story problems again.

"You know, a confederate." I shake my head. "Roosa." Exasperation lays heavy in his voice and manner. "I've seen the battle in your country years ago where those who didn't want to follow the rules fought against others in your battlefields." I have no idea what he's talking about. "They wore gray uniforms and fought against ones wearing blue uniforms."

I burst out laughing and fall to my knees. Tut scowls at me. "No, No! Oh, forgive me for laughing. I'm so sorry. It's just that," I break up again. Standing up, I swallow hard to keep myself under control. "Oh, Tut. I'm sorry."

"I don't know what is so funny about your people fighting their own people."

"No, it isn't that. It's...it's that the word you're searching for to describe him is rebel, not confederate." I choke back more laughter. "The words confederate rebels were used to describe the soldiers from the South." I can't stop myself and chuckle again. "He was a rebel. That's what you mean. Akhenaten was a rebel."

"Did the rebels not want to follow the rules of your country?"

I nod.

"Did the confederates not want to follow the rules of your country?"

I nod again.

"Then I do not see the problem with using either word to describe my father."

I stifle another laugh and nearly choke in the process. Tut continues to glare at me.

"No, you're right. But we use the word rebel."

"You have a strange world, Roosa. But to please you, he was a rebel and chose to have his tomb and those of the rest of the royal family built in these hills to catch the last light of the Aten each day."

"Oh." I say no more. Where does he get off calling my world strange? I've got other things to think about though and let it drop.

"Come, Roosa. We must climb." He starts up the path without waiting for me.

"Rebel." I chuckle to myself. "Who would have thought?"

The climb up the Amarna cliffs is grueling. Re beats down mercilessly. The path is barely there anymore. Once a well-traveled road, now the wind has blown the dust and sand away leaving rocks and boulders in our way. Clumps of pebbles litter our path at times causing each of us to lose our footing. It's comforting to see Tut struggle here too.

Stopping to take a short rest, I look back at the city. From this high up, it is hard to see where thousands of people once thrived or at least lived a mere thirty years ago. The pillars left standing at the palace entry look more like *Lincoln Logs* that were missed when cleaning up. The single bricks, still standing among the roads and living areas, fade into the ground. And there, beyond where the edge of the city lay, is the Nile, a striking contrast to the forgotten city before it.

Lush green reeds and papyrus line its banks,

visible even from here. Eucalyptus trees grow in small groves behind the reeds, preferring the dryer soil as opposed to the water-logged mud of the river bank. For some distance on both sides of the Nile, grasses and occasionally lotus flowers grow. Too small to see from the cliffs, but I saw those when we were first here just five days ago. It seems like forever. Beyond the grassland, for as far as I can see, the desert claims the land. I can make out some of the contours of the land that suggest dunes or formations of rocks sticking out of the desert floor.

"Roosa!"

I run to catch Tut. The reason for his excitement looms above us. Tombs are literally cut into the limestone cliffs. There are five.

"Which one?"

He points. "The middle one."

Nothing about the entrance signifies that it houses a pharaoh.

"It looks just like the others," I tell him. In fact, they all look like I took a pickaxe and just started digging.

"It was designed that way. The builders hoped to obscure its importance."

"Did a good job, if you ask me," I reply. Tut just gives me one of those teacher looks, and I smile back at him.

"You will see once we get inside."

For just a moment, I look once more behind me

at the Nile as it flows northward. The swift current is readily apparent even at this distance. I shiver in spite of the heat. Ghosts walking on my grave again, as Nana would say. We're being watched again. I can feel it. Reaching inside myself, I search for Hesena and come up with nothing. Are we too late?

I snap my head around to look at the path we climbed. No one is there. But I know now that Horemheb is lurking somewhere nearby. This is his last chance to stop us. It is where I would wait. He is here, either himself or his spirit, if that is even possible. He is here leaving evil in his path. He will not succeed. We will overpower him. His lies can't continue.

Tut is watching me strangely. "Nothing," I tell him. "Let's go and find Hesena."

Chapter 20

Picking our way down the corridor, the cool air is hard to breathe, like there's not enough oxygen in it or something.

The further away from the entrance, the more the odor of old death surrounds us. Tut carefully guards the flame of the torch we found at the entrance. If the light goes out, we will be unable to move; the darkness is so thick. We are forced to go slowly, testing each step. The incline is steep; one misstep could send us rushing to the bottom, wherever that is. Can't wait to make this trip back out.

Two passages cutting off the main corridor are blocked by large chunks of stone. It is eerie to see none of the color and decorations one would associate with a king's tomb. The walls here are bare just like the passages in Ay's tomb.

"Are we almost there?" The air grows thicker and colder. I shiver; it feels like I could reach out and touch the tension, it's so heavy here.

"Down this next set of stairs, and then past the

ritual well." He sounds distracted.

"There are no pictures. Why?"

"It is as my father wanted," he replies. "His burial chamber holds the Book of the Dead scenes and shows his devotion to the Aten."

Behind me I hear steps. Stopping, I peer back up the corridor, but all is silent. Hurrying to catch up, I run into Tut, who has halted.

"Oh, sorry." Then I see why he has stopped. All I can think is OMG.

Akhenaten's burial chamber lies in a shambles worse than Ay's. Broken jars are scattered everywhere. Sacred canopic jars that should have held the organs of the pharaoh: Pieces of figurines, the *shabtis*, lay scattered around the ground. Where Ay's burial chamber had been violated, Akhenaten's has been destroyed. Huge chunks of the walls lay on the floor. Only tiny bits of color cling to the walls. Nothing remains of a king here. Nothing but one thing.

I reach out to touch Tut. He swipes my hand away as if swatting a fly. I hear him speaking in the ancient tongue, the anger evident by the harsh sounding words and the pounding of his fist upon his chest.

There, in the center of the chamber, lies the granite sarcophagus which should contain Akhenaten's mummy. The heavy lid is in pieces on the ground. I walk past Tut who hasn't moved and look inside. My head swims, and the dizziness threatens to overtake me. The sarcophagus is empty.

Breathing in short gasps I kneel down to keep from falling and rest my head on the sarcophagus. The granite is cool and restores some equilibrium. My head still spins, and my brain's on overdrive.

Horemheb. He destroyed a pharaoh's tomb and took a pharaoh's mummy, an act denounced even in my time. Is this why Hesena has been silent? Has he destroyed her mummy also?

Tut's hand grips my shoulder.

"It is all right, Roosa. I should have expected this." He shakes his head. "She is still here somewhere, Roosa. I can feel it."

Strange that I cannot.

For several minutes we examine the tomb walls searching for something to indicate where Hesena rests. Nothing. If there is a false wall here, it's very well hidden.

"Tut," my voice croaks. Something is wrong. A force grips my throat. I fly through the air and hit the side of the sarcophagus. Blackness threatens to overcome me. I fight it. This is the showdown as I knew it would be. Horemheb is here.

Tut spins around as I land beside him. "Roosa!"

A wicked laugh echoes from the entryway. It is Horemheb in the flesh. Or, maybe in the spirit. I don't know, and I can't tell which. It is enough that he is here.

His shadow, cast by the torch he holds, looms

over us. He is a big man, a full two heads taller than Tut. He doesn't appear to have missed many meals either, although the muscles in his arms and legs show that he is no stranger to hard work. The double crown of Egypt sits upon his head as if molded to it.

"You should not have come here, Tutankhaten," Horemheb spits out. "Your family, you, and Ay are finished. Glorious Egypt will never acknowledge you as anything but traitors."

He turns his attention to me. My mouth drops open. I understand him!

"And you, you foolish girl. Did you really think that you could meddle in the affairs of the Pharaoh Horemheb? I gave you many warnings, but you did not heed them."

"You speak English! How? How can you?" I question.

"I'll tell you how, Roosa," Tut answers. "It is written all over the shadow of his *ba*. Seth has shared his evil powers with him. That is how he first saw us in the throne room of my father. What did you offer Seth for his magic, General?"

Horemheb stiffens at the informal address.

"I am Pharaoh Horemheb, boy. Seth will rule beside me and my sons and their sons. As it should be. Egypt will conquer the world as she should have done all along. The people will kneel at my feet, not spit upon them as they did your father's!"

Tut starts to advance. I stop him when I utter,

"Hesena."

"That's right, boy. Look for your precious queen. She will never be found. Her mummy, as well as Akhenaten's, was ordered destroyed by me. Pharaoh Horemheb. Nothing more will be heard from them, just as nothing will be heard from Ay. I not only deposed him in order to rule Egypt, I forbade him the Opening of the Mouth."

Tut glances at me with flashing eyes. I understand his message. Horemheb does not know that we have performed the ceremony.

"And I would have destroyed your mummy had I found it, boy. But I will correct that here." Horemheb smiles, showing his teeth which I swear are sharp and pointed like a crocodile. "Neither of you will leave here alive."

Well, that sucks. I'm the only one alive here now, at least I think so. Strange, I should be worried, but I'm not.

Horemheb continues to rant, and we let him, hoping, I hope, for Ay to appear from wherever he disappeared.

"I tell you, honor and respect shall not be given to Akhenaten or you or that fool, Ay. I've destroyed Ay's tomb, and men are on their way now to destroy his mummy. Forget being united with your queen. And you, Rosa? You will not be going home."

Is it also Seth's magic that lets him pronounce my name right? "We'll see about that," I say hoping to sound convincing. "What you've done is wrong, even evil. You cannot win."

Horemheb's laugh echoes again off the tomb walls. Then there is silence.

Chapter 21

My shoulders twitch, and I sense a presence behind me. Turning around, Ay stands there, his body glowing.

"You!" Horemheb spits out. Then he turns his anger on me. "Rosa, you shall pay for this with your life."

With a swiftness born of magic, Horemheb rushes by us grabbing my arm in the process. I am propelled in front of him as we pass by a startled Tut and Ay into the corridor. He attempts to stop my struggles by pressing my arm at an awkward angle behind my back.

I cry out in pain.

"It will only hurt for a small bit, foolish girl. You should have stayed in your own world."

He pushes me forward, making me stumble.

"Once outside I will end your meddling forever. The cliffs are high here, and you'll not survive the fall." His breathing is heavy as is mine. "Without your help, Ay would not have been found. Whatever part of

Ankhesenamun still lives in you will die also." He punctuates his words with a shove that sends me crashing into the granite wall. His laughter echoes my scream.

Determined not to be at his mercy, I turn and slap his face. He grabs my hands and lifts my body into the air.

"How dare you touch a Pharaoh of Egypt!"

"How dare *you* kill a Pharaoh of Egypt?" I shout back. And then with a power born of desperation, I lash out at him, my feet delivering swift kicks to his stomach; he drops me. Scrambling backwards on my hands and butt, I hardly notice the scrapes on my legs or the blood running down my face. Only when I wipe the moisture from my eyes do I realize there is blood on my hand.

Horemheb's whole body grows until his head reaches the top of the ceiling. It is the evil magic of Seth, the killer of his brother, Osiris.

"For that you shall die with my hands around your neck, you disrespectful servant!" He rushes toward me. At the last second I press my body flat against the wall. He stumbles past me. Regaining his balance he turns and prepares to attack again.

"Stop!"

We both freeze, our heads swiveling to find the one who spoke. Horemheb glowers at me, piercing the depths of my soul. No, our souls. I realize that Hesena has awakened inside of me.

"You will not harm this one."

"And who are you to stop me? Is this your magic, Rosa? If so, it will not work." He advances, and I try to back pedal, but my feet will not move.

"It is I, Ankhesenamun, Queen of Egypt, and you...you, who call yourself a Pharaoh of Egypt, will not put your hands on us again. May the Aten, Amun, and Re destroy you if you do."

"You do not frighten me, even if you are Ankhesenamun. I've killed one pharaoh already. I can kill you as easily."

"No, you cannot, Pharaoh Horemheb, although you no longer deserve that title," a voice from behind me speaks.

Turning I see Ay and Tut standing behind us. Ay restrains Tut with a hand on his arm.

"You can do nothing about this. You have no power in this time, Ay." He spits on the floor. "I did away with you once. Seth's magic will destroy your *ba* forever this time, and yours also, Tutankhaten."

Ay shakes his head sadly, but triumph sparkles in his old eyes.

They both step aside. Out of the shadows, the figures of several men walk. I hear Horemheb gasp and choke. Before us, coming from behind Ay and Tut, walk the priests of the Aten, Amun, and Re, each identified by the markings on their white robes: the sun surrounded by rays for the Aten, the eye of Horus as one with Amun, and the circle of Re. So that was where Ay went, to summon the priests.

Tut reaches out for me. In three long steps, I'm beside him, comfort and security warming my insides where only moments before ice formed. I lower my eyes. Deep inside I ask her forgiveness and wonder how I'll have the courage to leave his side and return home.

I feel a warmth deep inside, and a voice whispers to me.

"I understand, Rosa. I will give you the courage you need."

Tut pulls me closer. Does he even realize my heart is racing?

A bolt of light streaks out from the priests and brings Horemheb to his knees. I watch in horror as another being separates from his body. At least I think it's a body. A luminous shadow stands next to him, its face obscured by flashes of light.

I hear the chanting of the priests grow louder. They encircle Horemheb as their chants continue to increase in volume. The shadow lengthens, then contracts as it gets smaller and its light dims.

Horemheb cries out. "No!"

A priest of Re approaches the now translucent figure.

"Seth," he speaks. "You who saw fit to take Osiris' life will withdraw from the body of this Pharaoh. Vows he made to you will not be honored. You will go back to the Netherworld."

"No!" Horemheb cries out again. But the

combined power of the priests defeats Seth. His presence grows fainter until there is nothing left. Horemheb jumps to his feet as if to run, but the priests tighten their circle around him.

"Pharaoh Horemheb," the priest of Re who confronted Seth speaks. "At the Feast of Rejoicing, you will not name your son as your heir."

Horemheb blanches.

"If you do, your son will die before the next rising of Re."

I gasped. They would punish his son instead? I start to protest but Tut squeezes my hand hard, knowing what I am about to do. I look at Horemheb's broken form, his shoulders hunched over, not venturing a look at the priests.

"You will name the General Ramses to succeed you."

Horemheb stiffens at this but shows no other reaction.

"You have violated the Laws of the Gods by ending Ay's life with your hand. You will pay for that."

Horemheb raises his head, and there is real fear in his eyes. I grow afraid also, not knowing what else they will do.

"In the twenty-sixth year of your reign, you and your son will meet death."

My gasp is audible. Collectively, the priests glare at me. Tut jerks my arm, and Ay frowns at me.

Horemheb's head jerks up, and he jumps to his

feet. "You have no right to do such a thing." His voice echoes off the rock.

"You had no right to kill me," Ay responds. "I had already named you as my successor."

Tut arches his eyebrows.

"There was no one else equipped to lead the country," he answers Tut's unspoken question. Then he turns back to Horemheb. "You, you had only to wait until my death. I thought you had changed. I thought you had understood the reasons for what had come before."

"I understood that none of you were fit to rule Egypt and lead her people. Akhenaten was a fool who should never have been given the throne. Tut nothing but a boy who thought he could lead. Had you not died by your own foolish act, you would have met with a tragic accident."

I feel Tut's body shaking with anger. He starts toward him, but Ay holds out his arm to stop him.

"And you, Ay. Nothing more than a foolish old man who thought himself strong enough to rule beside the boy's queen. After her death, you became nothing." He pauses and appears to grow taller. "I did what had to be done for Egypt. I am not sorry for that. And if I am not to be Seth's vessel to restore Egypt to her glory once and for all, then so be it. His chance will come again." He looks each of us in the eye with a cold hard stare, and bowing ever so slightly to the priests, turns and walks away.

Chapter 22

I **stand there staring at nothing.** The priests follow Horemheb up the corridor. My legs begin to shake, and I crumple to the floor of the corridor. It's over. He can't try to kill me again. I will go home to my parents. Wrapping my arms around me, I try to stop the shakes. It is what I want, to go home.

I cringe as I recall the words of the priest of Re to Horemheb. I don't know what year this is of his reign, but he only has his death and that of his son to ponder. Tears prick at the corners of my eyes. The death of his son. To know he is the reason. How does one live with that? I can't imagine. This is not a world I want to live in.

A touch on my shoulder brings me back to the present. Tut, strong loving Tut, holds out his hand to me. Looking at his boyish body, I know now that this is no mere boy. This is truly a Pharaoh of an Egypt so powerful that it took strong leaders to rule her, even when those leaders were boys and girls. I spare a glance back toward the entrance, where he disappeared. I hang my head in sorrow.

"It is as it should be, Roosa. Egypt is a proud harsh land. Horemheb knew the consequences for his actions would be steep when he aligned himself with Seth. Nothing could change the path he took."

I nod. I can still feel the death grip of his hands on my arms.

"Come. Ay is ready to reveal Hesena's sarcophagus. The time is here to reclaim my Queen, my love."

I smile weakly, but knots are forming in my stomach. My biggest test is yet to come. Leaving.

.

Ay kneels at the foot of Akhenaten's empty sarcophagus. He is digging at the debris on the floor. A low rumble starts. The wall behind Ay seems to be moving. Impossible! Ay says something, and Tut leaves my side and rushes to the wall. A small vertical crack is showing down one side. Both Ay and Tut stand at the wall, fingers prying the crack wider. The rumble continues. Dust and the smell of grinding stone fill the tomb. It takes an eternity for the wall to move enough to reveal what it hides.

Tut and Ay step back from the building cloud, their arms slashing at the dust and coughing. It settles before reaching me on the far side of Akhenaten's sarcophagus.

We stare at what sits in the alcove: a pink granite

sarcophagus. Her sarcophagus. Goddess wings span each side protecting the Queen, just like the pictures in the books. Romeo said it best, "I ne'er saw true beauty til this night."

With gentle strokes, Tut brushes away the dust revealing the exquisite carving beneath. I move closer. Each of the wings is carved with perfection. The tip from one wing forms an unbroken connection with the adjoining one. The goddesses themselves are so exact that I wouldn't be surprised to see them come to life. Each strand of hair, each curl, each eye so detailed I am reminded of Sleeping Beauty waiting for a kiss to awaken her. I've seen pictures of sarcophagi and those of Tut, Ay, and Akhenaten, but nothing compares to this.

Tut hasn't said a word. His full concentration is focused on her. He and Ay are whispering now. I don't know why unless it is the reverence of this place. They both know that I can't understand the ancient language. Perhaps if Horemheb had performed the Opening of the Mouth, Ay would have been able to talk to me as Tut does, and Horemheb did through Seth's magic. But, if that were the case, none of this would have been necessary. I would just be that freak who holds conversations with dead people. Instead I'm far wiser than when Tut first came to me and I understand that my grandmother gave me a powerful gift. One I am now proud to have.

"Roosa," Tut bids me to come alongside

Hesena's final resting place. "Ay says you must embrace her sarcophagus as the goddesses do. You must let her *ba* that rests in you seek out and find her *ka* within."

He looks anxious, as if afraid I will refuse. I swallow hard, shaking a bit, but this is why I am here.

Ay guides me to one corner. Reverently he places first one hand on the left wing of the goddess. A chill runs through my body at his touch. Like a ghost walking over my grave. He is a ghost now, I realize, a complete ghost.

Tut takes my other hand and deftly places it on the right wing of the goddess, his touch sure and strong.

I stand there embracing her sarcophagus, fear hanging at the edge, fear that this will not work.

A gentle stirring comes from deep inside my body, from deep in my soul. Humbled, I lay my head against the goddess' head. A faint humming and a small vibration come from within the sarcophagus. A tingling reaches my fingertips and travels up my arms into the core of my being. A sharp intake of air escapes from my lips. My brain clouds. Nothing is clear. Fighting the dizziness, I close my eyes tight. And that is when it happens.

A light touch upon my forehead, fleeting as the kiss of morning dew in the rising sun. There, and gone. Then...she speaks.

"Thank you, Rosa. I know the sacrifices you have made

for us, even if Tut Khan does not. You shall ever be a part of us. May Isis forever guide your soul and one day bring you back to us."

Opening my eyes, I wipe away the tears before they fall. Tut helps me up.

"Did you...is she?"

"Yes, Roosa. You did it. Thank you." His eyes sparkle with happiness, but I sense something else.

"What?"

"I was afraid, Roosa. Afraid as I have been only two other times in my life that this would not work." He embraces me for the last time. "Thank you."

"Can I...see her?"

He turns to his right side. "She is here. Look upon my Queen and my love."

Nervously I search beside him. I see nothing. Wait. There, a glimmer. Then she stands before me. Her striking features are more beautiful in person. Her shining black hair falls down around her face and shoulders. Around her neck a gold chain glitters. It holds a golden Ankh, the symbol of Life. Black kohl around her emerald eyes intensifies their depths. Her lips are touched with just a hint of red dye. Golden bracelets hang on her wrists and sparkle off the jewels embroidered on her white sheath. Small golden sandals cover her tiny feet. I've never seen so much gold on one person, and probably never will again, at least not the real kind. She is beyond beautiful. She bows her head to me and smiles.

Looking around, there is no one else in the chamber. Turning to Tut, I start to speak, but he anticipates my question.

"Ay gives you his thanks. He has gone on now to a restful peace at last."

"Oh." Thought he might have stuck around a bit. Tut clears his throat.

"Roosa, there are no words for you that express our gratitude. What you have done for Hesena and I knows no tangible reward. As for my father, Ay, and myself, you have restored our honor as all will see." He kneels at my feet and takes my hand. Putting it to his lips, he kisses it. My heart skips, and then calms itself. "We will never forget what you have done. You have restored the Sons of the Sphinx to their rightful place in Egyptian history. Thank you."

He rises and waits for me to speak. For maybe the second time in my life, I don't know what to say.

"Tut, I...I," My words refuse to come. Looking into his ebony eyes I realize once more that I have done what is right for all of us. "Tut," I start again. "Thank you." A questioning look comes over his face. "You have made me realize that whatever this power is that my grandmother passed to me, it is above all else a gift."

He smiles that lopsided smile.

"A gift that I was given. It allowed me to enter into your world, your life, and I will treasure that."

I'm not good at goodbyes, and I know that is

what this is. He is not coming back with me. That is as it should be. They will be together for all of eternity now. Somehow Tut understands how difficult this is for me, as he has understood me all through this journey.

"One last time I must send you through the time wrap, Roosa. You will find that only minutes have gone by in your time."

Minutes. A lifetime it seems.

"Re will not allow me to go with you. Truth is I have no wish to leave Hesena's side ever again." At his loving glance, she holds out her hand. He takes what she offers. "We would like to give you a gift to take back to your world."

A gift from a Pharaoh and his Queen. My gift from the Window of Appearances. Holding out my hand, Tut shakes his head. He reaches around behind me, and I feel a warmth against my chest. I look down and gasp. Quickly I look to Hesena's neck. She tilts her head, and her green eyes sparkle. Around my neck Tut has clasped her gold chain with the golden Ankh. Its warmth courses through my body and my hand when I finger it.

"Come, give me your hand, Roosa."

I take one last look around, imprinting Hesena's pink granite sarcophagus on my memory. I grasp his hand thinking that he never did learn to say my name right.

Tut's other hand lifts my chin. He leans over; his

breath tickles my ear as he whispers.

"I do know the sacrifices you have made," he whispers. "All of them, Rosa."

Then before I can respond, his lips touch mine, and my world spins.

Glossary of Egyptian Gods, People, Places, and Terms

Gods

Amun-Re—King of the Gods; Amun (creator god) combined with Re (sun god).

Anubis—Depicted as a jackal, god of mummification and guardian of tombs.

Aten—Sun disc worshipped by Akhenaten (Amenhotep IV) which replaced Amun-Re.

Geb—God of the earth.

Horus—Falcon god of the sky; son of Isis and Osiris; defeated evil Seth.

Isis—Goddess of magic; wife of Osiris and mother of Horus.

Nut—Goddess of the Sky.

Osiris—God of the Underworld; murdered by brother Seth; body parts strewn throughout Egypt.

Re—God of the Sun; journeys through the Underworld each night.

Seth—God of Chaos; murdered his brother Osiris; defeated by Horus.

Thoth—God of Wisdom; represented most often by a baboon.

People

Akhenaten (Amenhotep IV)—Father of Tutankhamen; considered a renegade for worshipping the Aten and not Amun; married to Nefertiti.

Amenhotep III—Father of Akhenaten; grandfather of Tutankhamen; married to Tiye.

Ankhesenamun—Daughter of Akhenaten and Nefertiti; married to Tutankhamen.

Ay—Father of Nefertiti; grandfather of Ankhesenamun.

Horemheb—General of the Egyptian armies under Akhenaten; supposedly married Nefertiti's sister so he could become pharaoh.

Khufu (Cheops)—Pharaoh 2575-2528 BC; his burial site is the largest pyramid on the Giza Plateau and one of the ancient wonders of the world.

Nefertiti—Daughter of Ay, wife of Akhenaten, and mother of Ankhesenamun; thought to have ruled Egypt during the end of Akhenaten's rule.

Tutankhamen—Son of Akhenaten; mother is not known; referred to as The Boy King; married Ankhesenamun; tomb discovered in 1922 by Howard Carter.

Places

Akhet-Aten—The city that Akhenaten founded north of Thebes; also known as el-Armana.

Giza Plateau—Located near the ancient capital of Memphis and the modern capital city of Cairo; contains the three pyramids and the Sphinx; west of the Nile.

Nile River—The life blood of Egypt; runs the entire length of the country and all agriculture depends on it for water, as does the entire population of Egypt.

Thebes (Luxor)—Ancient name for the city of Luxor; capital city during the New Kingdom; location of Karnak Temple where pharaohs were crowned including Tutankhaten; on the east bank of the Nile.

Valley of the Kings—The Royal Necropolis; burial place for the New Kingdom pharaohs.

Western Valley—An extension to the west of the Valley of the Kings; contains only four burials (so far discovered) including Ay's.

Terms

Anhk—Symbol of Everlasting life; represented by a cross with a loop on top.

ba—The spiritual part of a person's soul sometimes referred to as the breath of life or the life force; undertakes a journey through the afterlife before uniting with the ka.

Canopic jars—Ceramic containers for the internal organs of the dead with lids in the shape of the head of one of the Four Sons of Horus who protected the organs: Hapi, a baboon, guarded the lungs; Duamutef, a jackal, guarded the stomach; Imseti, a human, guarded the liver; and Qebehsenuef, a falcon, guarded the intestines.

Cartouche—Hieroglyphic representation of the names of pharaohs and other members of royalty written inside an oval.

Cubit—An Egyptian measure of length or depth in the ancient world. One royal cubit was equal to the length of a man's arm from the elbow to the extended fingertips, approximately 52.4 cm or about 20 inches.

Duat—The journey made by Re each night in order to be reborn the following day. The journey carried the god through the twelve hours of the night. Also the passage followed by a pharaoh's *ba* in order to reach the afterlife and be reborn.

Eye of Horus—Resembles the eye of a falcon and represents the right eye of the Egyptian falcon god Horus; according to legend, the left eye was torn from Horus by his uncle Seth and restored by Thoth, the god of magic and wisdom; Eye of Horus was believed to have healing and protective power and often used as a protective amulet; also known as the Eye of Re (Udjat, Wedjat).

ka—The life force of a person; remained in the tomb until united with the ba.

Maat (Ma'at)—Represented the order of the Egyptian world; pharaohs were to maintain Maat in order for the people to exist and prosper.

Opening of the Mouth—An elaborate ritual preformed in the tomb which enabled the mummy to partake of food and drink in the afterlife.

Pyramids—Burial monuments for pharaohs; most well-known are the Pyramids on the Giza Plateau: Khufu (Wonder of the Ancient World), his son Khafre, and his grandson Menkaure.

Sarcophagus—The granite (usually) container of the mummy of the dead; Tutankhamen's red granite sarcophagus was found inside of four elaborately decorated, gilded (golden) shrines.

Scarab—Actually a dung beetle which laid eggs in a ball of dung and then rolled it around the ground to ensure even heating for the babies; emergence of babies represented rebirth; linked to Khepri, a creator god which presented the sun god Re as he rose each morning.

Sphinx—A crouching lion or lioness with a human head; most famous and recognizable sphinx is found on the Giza Plateau.

Stele—Slabs of stone or wood used in ancient Egypt on which boundaries were denoted, messages from pharaohs were written, and special events or happenings were noted; written in hieroglyphs.

To My Readers:

If you liked *Sons of the Sphinx*, please be kind enough to leave a short review on the site where you purchased the book. I hope you share your reading enjoyment with friends and family.

Want to know more about Tutankhamen? Try my historical fiction book *Tutankhamen Speaks*.

Connect with me on Facebook at Author Cheryl Carpinello, on my blog Carpinello's Writing Pages (http://carpinelloswritingpages.blogspot.com), and on my website Beyond Today Educator (http://www.beyondtodayeducator.com).

I, Fiona Ingram, and Wendy Leighton-Porter would like to invite you to our new site:

The Quest Books:
http://adventurequestbooks.com

At The Quest Books, you will find adventure, excitement, and mystery from across the Ancient and Medieval Worlds for MG/Tween/YA readers. Sign up for our newsletter to be one of the first to receive notice of new books and events.

Coming in 2015

The long awaited sequel to *Guinevere: On the Eve of Legend*. Don't miss the further adventures of Guinevere and Cedwyn in *Guinevere: At the Dawn of Legend*.